"I'm so sorry," Lark said quickly as the phone vibrated again. "But I really need to get this. It's my daughter's nanny." She bent to pick the phone up off the table, turning as she looked down at it.

He could see the screen over her shoulder. On it was a photo of a baby, a little girl dressed in pink. She had a cloud of soft rose-gold curls and blue, blue eyes.

It was a singular color that rose gold, as was the intense blue of her eyes. He'd never met anyone else who'd had hair that hue apart from his mother. And as for that blue...

That was Donati blue. Two hundred years ago the Donatis had been patrons of a painter who'd created a paint color in their honor. And that's what he'd called it.

Cesare went very still as everything in him slowed down. Everything except his brain, which was now working overtime. Going back over that night. Going over everything.

Because if there was one thing he knew, it was that the baby in that photo was his daughter.

Scandalous Heirs

Two impulsive nights of passion...
Two positive pregnancy tests!

Billionaires and friends Cesare and Aristophanes have both vowed never to let *anything* distract them from their work. Distractions can only lead to ruin. But neither can resist making the most dangerous mistake of all—giving in to desire for two alluring women. The consequences? Claiming their one-night heirs!

Cesare is haunted by the memories of the mystery woman he spent one night of passion with. Two years later, they meet again in Italy by chance, and he makes a shocking discovery—she's secretly had his baby daughter, but she can't remember who he is!

Read all about it in

Italian Baby Shock

Available now!

When Aristophanes meets preschool teacher Nell, they agree to one searing yet unforgettable night together—no strings attached. Until he finds her on his doorstep months later with a shocking revelation... She's carrying his twins!

Coming soon!

ITALIAN BABY SHOCK

JACKIE ASHENDEN

PRESENTS

Recycling programs for this product may not exist in your area.

ISBN-13: 978-1-335-93915-9

Italian Baby Shock

For questions and comments about the quality of this book, please contact us at CustomerService@Harlequin.com.

Harlequin Enterprises ULC
22 Adelaide St. West, 41st Floor
Toronto, Ontario M5H 4E3, Canada
www.Harlequin.com

Printed in Lithuania

Jackie Ashenden writes dark, emotional stories with alpha heroes who've just gotten the world to their liking only to have it blown apart by their kick-ass heroines. She lives in Auckland, New Zealand, with her husband, the inimitable Dr. Jax, two kids and two rats. When she's not torturing alpha males and their gutsy heroines, she can be found drinking chocolate martinis, reading anything she can lay her hands on, wasting time on social media or being forced to go mountain biking with her husband. To keep up-to-date with Jackie's new releases and other news, sign up to her newsletter at jackieashenden.com.

Books by Jackie Ashenden

Harlequin Presents

The Innocent's One-Night Proposal
The Maid the Greek Married
His Innocent Unwrapped in Iceland
A Vow to Redeem the Greek
Spanish Marriage Solution

Rival Billionaire Tycoons

A Diamond for My Forbidden Bride
Stolen for My Spanish Scandal

Three Ruthless Kings

Wed for Their Royal Heir
Her Vow to Be His Desert Queen
Pregnant with Her Royal Boss's Baby

The Teras Wedding Challenge

Enemies at the Greek Altar

Visit the Author Profile page
at Harlequin.com for more titles.

For my King of Cups

CHAPTER ONE

HER PHONE VIBRATED yet again but Lark Edwards tried not to look at it. It was nothing. Maya had a little cold, that was all. It wasn't life-threatening. It didn't require hospitalisation. The nanny who was looking after her for the night held qualifications in child health and was more than capable of looking after a fifteen-month-old with the sniffles.

If anything was gravely wrong, she'd contact Lark immediately, she'd promised.

Lark's fingers closed tightly around the phone.

She always tried to look on the bright side of things and stay positive, but perhaps there *was* something gravely wrong. Perhaps that's why her phone was vibrating. Perhaps Maya had suddenly become very ill and the nanny was trying to contact her to tell her.

Lark took a breath, calmed her racing heartbeat and gave herself a mental slap.

No. It was fine. She was only wound up because this was the first time she'd been away from Maya longer than a day. Mr Ravenswood, her boss, who owned Ravenswood Antiques, one of London's most exclusive antique businesses, had taken ill with the flu and hadn't been able to travel, so he'd asked Lark to go to Italy in his stead.

It was a very important assignment, he'd said, and it was vital someone from Ravenswood go. And since she was the only one who was free, it had to be her. She didn't have his knowledge of antiques since she was only his personal assistant, not to mention only being in the job a year, but he'd been giving her some basic training in the business for the past six months, and she was at least a little familiar with Italy, having been there once before. Also, all she'd have do, he'd assured her, was to view the pieces that the Donati family were wanting to sell to ascertain they were genuine—he'd told her what to look for—and to take as many pictures as she could.

It would have been easier for someone on the Donati end to send the pictures without the need to travel, but Mr Ravenswood had been adamant that someone had to view the items personally. Also, they were to speak to Signor Donati himself, since Ravenswood Antiques prided themselves on the personal touch. Mr Ravenswood had been very upset about the illness that had prevented him from flying to Rome. Then again, he couldn't ask such an important and busy man such as Signor Donati to rearrange his schedule purely for the sake of an old antiques dealer.

Also, the Donati pieces were special and could earn the business a lot of money, and Mr Ravenswood didn't want to do anything that might jeopardise the sale.

Lark had felt sorry for him. Jasper Ravenswood had given her a job just after Maya had been born and she'd been despairing of ever finding someone who'd employ a new mother. But he'd given her a position, and hadn't complained when she'd had to bring Maya into the office. So it was only the right thing to do to agree to go to Rome, see the pieces and talk to Mr Donati herself.

Jasper had been so effusively thankful, he'd paid for the very expensive nanny to look after Maya, Lark's daughter, for the night.

Lark took another calming breath.

Yes, it was only a night and Maya wasn't a little baby any more. The nanny, Emily, had been lovely too. She just had to stay positive.

As if determined to ruffle her calm, her phone vibrated once again and this time Lark couldn't resist having a quick look. But it was only a text from Mr Ravenswood wishing her good luck.

She smiled, typed in a quick thank you, then put the phone down on the overly gilded table in front of her, and forced herself to relax.

It could be just being in Italy again that was messing with her usually positive outlook, or maybe it was sitting on this beautiful velvet-covered couch—no doubt another antique worth thousands of euros—in this beautiful room, in the beautiful, centuries-old Donati palazzo just outside of Rome that was getting to her.

It wasn't all that conducive to relaxation.

It definitely *wasn't* being in Italy again. That night had been two years ago now, so if not the *distant* past, then very much *not* the recent past. It had no bearing on the future and she certainly never thought of that night in particular, not if she could help it.

She always tried to stay positive.

Leaning against the stiff back of the sofa, Lark looked around the salon—or so the member of the Donatis' house staff had called it, definitely not anything as common as a 'lounge'—and it was huge. The rust-red silk-panelled walls looked as if they had been hand painted and were hung with huge paintings of battle scenes in gilt frames. There seemed to be a lot of gilt on the ornate plaster cornices too, as well as on the intricately painted ceiling.

The parquet on the floor was ancient and worn and covered with hand-knotted silk rugs, while the armchairs and couch she sat on were velvet covered and as gilded as the old and huge fireplace that Lark sat in front of. Chandeliers hung from the ceiling and above the fireplace hung a massive portrait of two people in modern dress, which looked out of place with the rest of the room's stately opulence. A handsome man with cold blue eyes stood beside a seated woman with beautiful red-gold curls. Neither of them looked particularly happy and it somehow made the room seem dark and vaguely oppressive. Though that could have been due to the heavy dark blue silk curtains partially concealing the windows.

Not a place to slump on the sofa with a tub of ice cream and a glass of wine while watching movies on one's laptop, that was for sure. Which was exactly what she was going to do back at her hotel once she'd finished looking at the pieces Mr Ravenswood had wanted her to look at, taken the photos she'd been instructed to take and talked nice to whichever Donati family representative she was supposed to talk to.

Tomorrow she'd fly back to London and her daughter. It was only a night, not a big deal.

She smoothed the fuchsia-pink skirt she wore and double-checked she hadn't spilled anything on her blouse.

It was new and patterned with roses that matched the fuchsia of her skirt, and she loved it—wearing bright and cheerful colours always made her feel good. Luckily, there were no incriminating stains, which surprised her since being the mother of a young child meant clothing got stained on a regular basis and usually in mysterious circumstances.

It wouldn't do to appear untidy though, not today, not when she was here on behalf of Ravenswood Antiques. Mr Ravenswood had a certain reputation to uphold and she was determined to uphold it. He'd also been very clear that the Donatis weren't just any old Italian family. They owned Donati Bank, a private banking company that had been founded around six hundred years earlier, while the family's legacy went back even further. They were one of the oldest and most important families in Italy, their history and wealth equalling and even surpassing some of Europe's royal families.

It wasn't exactly a bright history, however.

Lark had done some research on the plane to Rome and the Donati family had been notorious in the Renaissance for all kinds of poisonings and stabbings. They'd had a thing for assassinations apparently, targeting anyone they viewed as a threat to their family. There wasn't any of that nowadays, of course, but their reputation in the business world was still as ruthless as it had been back in the day. Mostly courtesy of Cesare Donati, the last Donati heir, who drove the business like a racing car driver on the track. Fast and hard and with an aim to win.

He was an imposing, almost mythical figure, with a head for money and a reach in the finance world that spanned the globe, Donati Bank having offices in all the major financial hubs. He advised governments, held the accounts of many global corporations, as well as the personal accounts of some of the wealthiest people in the world, and had a reputation for being as ruthless as the Donatis of old.

She hoped the assistant she'd dealt with had passed on to him that he'd be meeting her instead of Mr Ravenswood. She hoped he wouldn't mind too much. He might even be too busy to meet with her, which would be fine since she didn't relish the thought of having to deal with a man like him. Her own father had been wealthy and powerful, and she and her mother had spent years running from him, so she knew what that type of man could be like.

Then again, she was good with people, and anyway, maybe speaking to Signor Donati would only take a few minutes. Maybe this whole thing would only take an hour or so, and then she might even be able to change her flight and leave Rome tonight. The flights had been full when she'd last checked, but being waitlisted was a possibility. Then she would get back to London and be there for when Maya woke up the next morning.

That was a bolstering thought and she felt much better, until her phone vibrated on the table again. She reached out to grab it, just as the salon's ornate double doors opened and a man stepped in the room. He closed them with a brisk click then turned to her.

And Lark's breath caught in her throat.

He was exceedingly tall—almost a foot taller than her modest five foot four—and powerfully muscled, the width and breadth of his shoulders and chest emphasised by the perfectly tailored dark suit he wore.

He was also beautiful, his face a work of art in the sculpted planes and angles of cheekbones, nose and forehead. His hair was black and short, the same colour as his winged eyebrows and sooty lashes, all of which made the deep, piercing blue of his eyes even more astonishing.

The same piercing blue of the man in the painting above the fireplace. Though unlike the painting, this man brought a crackling energy and force into the room, as if a fierce storm had come through the doors after him.

For a second Lark sat there, her phone forgotten, utterly transfixed.

She'd seen his face in many media articles, both online and in print. It was instantly recognisable. But that crackling energy he'd brought with him, the magnetism of his physical presence, made him completely unforgettable. And utterly mesmerising.

It was Cesare Donati, head of Donati Bank.

Her mouth dry, her heart pounding, Lark pushed herself to her feet, trying to resist the urge to wipe her sweaty palms down her skirt. She felt self-conscious all of a sudden, deeply aware that she was here as Mr Ravenswood's representative and yet not knowing a great deal about antiques. She'd learned a lot in the past six months, but that wasn't the same as someone who had a lot of experience in the field. And no doubt Signor Donati would expect her to have a lot of experience.

Well, there was nothing to be done about that now. She'd just have to be her normal bright, cheerful self, and hopefully that would be enough. He was a human being like any other and most human beings liked her.

Apparently, according to her mother, her smile could heal the world.

Signor Donati's attention was on his phone as he stopped near the couch, typing a message out to someone before slipping the phone back into the pocket of his impeccably tailored suit trousers. Then he looked at her and those piercing blue eyes of his widened, a look of shock rippling over his handsome face. He stared at her as if he'd seen a ghost.

Her heart was already beating far too fast and she had no idea why he was looking at her that way—perhaps he hadn't been informed that Mr Ravenswood wouldn't be here? Regardless, being friendly always put people at their ease, so she took a step towards him and held out a hand.

'*Buongiorno*, Signor Donati,' she said in her hastily practised and atrocious Italian. Then, switching to English, she went on, 'I hope my message was passed on? I know you were expecting Mr Ravenswood, but unfortunately he was unable to come due to illness, and he sent me in his stead. My name is Lark Edwards and it's a great pleasure to meet you.'

Cesare Donati made no move to take her hand. In fact, he didn't move at all. He only stared at her, his gaze twin spears of sapphire pinning her in place. 'You,' he murmured, his voice deep, rich and full of shock. 'What the hell are *you* doing here?'

Lark blinked. He'd said it as if he knew her, which was strange, because she'd never met him. She'd remember if she had, very definitely.

'Uh…me?' she asked uncertainly. 'Well, as I said, Mr Ravenswood was sick so I—'

'I told you there would be no contact between us,' he

interrupted and then took an abrupt step towards her, his gaze sweeping over her as if he was meticulously recording every aspect of her appearance. 'I told you not to go looking.'

Lark blinked again, her surprise deepening into confusion. 'I'm sorry,' she said carefully, not wanting to offend him. 'Have we…met before? Or perhaps you've mistaken me for someone else?'

He said nothing. His fallen angel features were drawn tight to the perfect bone structure of his face, his beautifully carved mouth hard. A muscle leapt in his impressive jaw, his astonishing blue eyes studying her so intently she felt almost consumed by them.

A disturbing heat bloomed inside her, making her skin prickle and her breath catch yet again. It was physical attraction, she knew that, but a worse man to be attracted to she couldn't imagine, and not only because he'd never be interested in someone like her. He was also the very epitome of all she disliked about the male species: rich, arrogant and entitled, and even if he had been interested in her, she would have avoided him like the plague.

You did like one man, remember?

Yes. Maya's father. Except the problem was that she *didn't* remember.

Oh, she remembered her mother's death from cancer and then the dreary London winter that had felt as if it would never end. Then that fateful trip to Italy she'd taken to cheer herself up. And she remembered her handbag getting stolen in Rome but…the next thing she knew she'd woken up in hospital. Apparently she'd been hit by a car crossing the street and had banged her head hard, though she had no memory of it. No memory of the night she'd had either.

But she must have spent it with a man, because nine months later, Maya was born.

At first, she'd dismissed that night, because she hadn't had any long-term injuries and she seemed to be fine. But then, when the fact of her pregnancy had become apparent, she'd been terrified, and no amount of looking on the bright side and being positive had helped.

That her baby was healthy according to the midwife made no difference. She'd always wanted children, but hadn't expected to have them so soon let alone not have the slightest idea who'd fathered her child. In the end she'd visited a psychologist to talk through her fears, because no matter how her baby had been conceived, there was no doubting Lark would be a mother and she wanted to be the best mother she could be. She wanted to keep her baby and love it when it was born. The psychologist had helped, and after a few sessions, Lark had decided that her pregnancy wasn't something to fear. It was a last mystical gift from her mother, a blessing even. Because a blessing was exactly what a child was.

But there was no possibility though, that the man she'd spent the night with was this man. None whatsoever. She'd remember if she had, she was positive. He was so memorable in every conceivable way; it was impossible *not* to remember him.

Lark dropped her outstretched hand and gave him her brightest smile instead. 'Well,' she said. 'If I could just have a look at these pieces your representatives talked to us about and perhaps take a few photos, then I'll get out of your hair.'

* * *

It was *her.* There was no doubt. No doubt at all.

Cesare stood in the middle of his family's centuries-old salon, very conscious of the blood pumping hard in his veins and the shock that rippled like an earthquake through him.

It had been nearly two years ago, but he still remembered that night as if it had been yesterday.

The aunt who'd brought him up after his parents had died had just passed away after a heart attack, which meant he was now the last of the Donati line, and even though he'd been determined not to let that bother him in any way, it had. He'd gone out walking the streets, sending his bodyguards away because he'd craved solitude. They hadn't been happy about it, but since he was the boss and they valued their jobs, they did what they were told.

He'd walked for hours, telling himself he felt nothing, that the toxic combination of grief and fury in his gut didn't exist, and he'd been on the point of finding a bar to make sure the embers of it were well and truly drowned, when he'd come across a tourist who'd just had her handbag stolen. She hadn't spoken any Italian and she'd been upset. She hadn't recognised him, either, and though he didn't normally go out of his way to help people—he'd inherited his parents' selfish natures and he knew it—when she'd burst out that she'd just lost her mother, he knew he couldn't leave her on her own.

So he'd mobilised his staff to help her and while they'd dealt with the police, the banks, and the British embassy for a replacement passport, he'd taken her out to dinner. She'd had no money and was hungry, and he needed the distraction.

And what a distraction she'd proven to be, with her wealth of honey gold hair and beautiful sea-green eyes. He'd always had his pick of beautiful women, and while she wasn't who he'd normally choose for a partner, he'd found himself drawn to her all the same. She'd been so expressive and open, and even in the midst of her grief, she'd smiled. It had been the most astonishing smile he'd ever seen in his entire life, warm and generous and utterly sincere. No one had ever smiled at him that way and it felt like the most precious gift he'd ever been given.

Lark, she'd said her name was. Like the bird.

She hadn't had anywhere to go that night, and so he'd offered her a guest room in his villa. They'd sat up till midnight talking in the library and then the chemistry he'd felt all night and yet tried to ignore had sparked and ignited. And she'd been just as warm and expressive and sincere in bed as she had been during their dinner. Passionate too. Giving herself to him with an abandon that had spoken of deep trust. Another precious gift.

She hadn't known him, yet she'd trusted him with her body implicitly.

He'd never had a night with a woman with whom he'd felt such a connection.

It couldn't go anywhere, of course. Because by then he'd already decided that the toxicity of the Donati line would end with him. Selfish, his parents would have called it, and yes, it was. Petty and selfish, revenge for a childhood where he hadn't been a child so much as a possession to be fought over and used. A weapon his parents had aimed at each other.

They'd done their best to leave their scars on him, but he'd refused to be marked. And as for the legacy they'd thought had been so important, well… He could be as petty and selfish as they once had been.

He'd break up the precious Donati legacy, sell it off bit by bit, even Donati bank would go. He'd never marry, never have children. There would be no one else to take the name, no one else to shoulder the weight of that toxic history, no one else to ensure the whole bitter bloodline carried on.

Once he was dead, so were the Donatis.

Anyway, he'd made sure she knew that it would be one night and only one, and the next day, he'd left her sleeping in his bed. By the time he'd got home that evening, she was gone. He'd never heard from her again.

Until today.

Now, here she was, standing in the middle of the salon, dressed in a tight-fitting pink skirt and a blouse with roses on it, outrageously pretty and colourful in his overwrought, overdecorated palazzo. Giving him that beautiful smile he remembered and yet looking at him as if she had no idea who he was. As if she hadn't spent an entire night, writhing in pleasure in his arms. He didn't understand. How could she have forgotten?

'Don't you know who I am?' he demanded before he could stop himself. Something he'd never had to ask because people always knew who he was.

Her big green eyes widened and a small crease appeared between her brows. 'Of course I do. You're Signor Donati, head of Donati Bank.'

He waited for her to add something more, something

along the lines of 'yes, of course I remember the night we spent together, how could I forget that?' But she didn't.

Perhaps she didn't recognise him as the man she'd spent the night with, though again, surely that was impossible. They'd spent hours in each other's company, just talking. Then yet more hours not talking at all, only touching, kissing, tasting. Giving pleasure and receiving it. Did she not remember that?

Apart from anything else, he was head of the largest and oldest private bank in Europe, if not the entire world, and everything he did was the stuff of rumour and gossip. He couldn't go anywhere without being photographed by the paparazzi. Entire governments asked for his financial advice.

He was recognised everywhere and more than one woman who'd spent the night with him had sold their story to different news organisations around the globe.

All those stories were, without exception, glowing.

It was impossible that this particular woman didn't remember him. Unless, of course, she wasn't the woman he'd spent the night with… But no, he was certain she was the one. She'd said her name was Lark and it wasn't that common a name.

Yet, she was looking at him as if he was a total stranger.

Annoyance wound through him and it wasn't wounded pride, absolutely not. Merely irritation. He'd been expecting Ravenswood, not her, and that she just happened to be a woman he'd slept with a long time ago wasn't something he'd expected to have to deal with. It wasn't of note, though. And if she didn't remember him, he certainly wasn't going to tell her.

He'd been very clear, after all, that they'd only have a night and that there would be no further contact and she'd been in agreement. And up until this moment she'd been as good as her word.

Perhaps she was here because she'd wanted to see him? And pretending not to recognise him? Then again, why would she bother? And what had she said about Ravenswood?

Annoyed that his shock at her arrival had meant that he hadn't taken in anything she'd said, Cesare pulled himself together. Emotional control was vital and he couldn't let her unexpected appearance get to him. He was the head of Donati Bank, for God's sake, not a teenage boy with his first crush.

He gave her a cool look. 'Yes,' he said. 'That's exactly who I am. And as head of Donati Bank, I expected to see Mr Ravenswood himself not you.'

Her smile didn't falter. 'I know, but Mr Ravenswood has had a terrible bout of flu and he wasn't in any condition to travel. He also didn't want anyone to rearrange their schedule because of him, so he asked me if I'd be willing to look at your items on his behalf.'

She was still smiling warmly and shock was still bouncing around inside him, and he was aware that a very male part of him was noting how low the neckline of her blouse was, and how it showed off her pretty creamy skin as well as the dips and hollows of her collarbone. Skin he'd spent a long time tasting. Dips and hollows he'd spent a long time tracing with his tongue. In fact, he'd spent a long time following every line of that delectable, curvy body of hers with his hands and his mouth, and he'd relished every cry he'd brought from her. She'd smelled of vanilla, he remembered, like a sweet confection, making his mouth water…

He shoved the erotic memories aside, ignored the sudden increase in his blood pressure. No, he should *not* be thinking about that night. It was over and done with, and no matter how pretty this woman was, and no matter that she didn't recognise him, he wasn't going to let either of those things affect him.

It had only been physical attraction, nothing more, and he'd never let something as banal as lust rule him. He was in complete control of himself as he was in complete control of everything else he did, and while he'd enjoyed that one night, he wasn't going to pursue another. He'd never needed to chase a woman and he wasn't about to start.

'And who exactly are you?' he asked tightly.

She gave him that bright, sunny smile again. 'Oh, I'm Mr Ravenswood's personal assistant.'

'And do you know anything about antiques?'

'Not as much as he does, it's true.' This time her smile was self-deprecating. 'But I've been training with him for the past six months and he's told me what to look for. I'll also be taking some photos if that's okay.'

His annoyance, already simmering, deepened. He'd given up some of his precious time to oversee this particular matter himself. The pieces were valuable, dating from the Renaissance, and were worth a lot of money.

He was going to sell them—he was going to sell *everything* in the palazzo—and donate the money to charity, so he wanted to get the best price he could and that meant having them appraised accurately. He'd already had the list of charities he was going to donate to drawn up and all of them his father would have disapproved of. That satisfied him unreasonably.

What did not satisfy him was having his one-night stand turn up at his palazzo and apparently not remember that she slept with him. It shouldn't matter to him and yet for some reason it did.

'If all that was required were some pictures, I could have taken them myself,' he snapped.

Generally, when he took that tone, people leapt to either do his bidding or apologise for whatever transgression they'd made, but Lark merely gave him another of those pretty, sunny smiles, as though she hadn't heard the annoyance in his voice.

'Oh, no, that's not necessary,' she said soothingly. 'Mr Ravenswood was very insistent that I view them personally. Again, I'm so sorry you were inconvenienced. All you have to do is show me where the pieces are and I can do the rest.'

She really was very pretty, with a delicate nose and chin, and a perfect little rosebud of a mouth. And her expression radiated warmth and openness, her sea-green eyes sparkling.

It was as if a shaft of summer sunlight had suddenly illuminated the room, making everything feel lighter and brighter. Not so cold and oppressive and…dark.

She made him remember that night, the warmth he'd felt radiating from her, the way she'd opened her arms to him, welcoming him with such passion. And how no matter what he told himself, he had never forgotten her…

He didn't like it. He didn't want it.

Just then something vibrated on the small seventeenth-century table in front of the sofa. It was a phone, the screen lighting up.

The smile on Lark's face faltered, her expression tightening.

So, it was her phone. And clearly she was distracted by it.

His decision, already half made, solidified into certainty. He didn't want her here; she was distracting and he couldn't afford to be distracted now, not when he had so much to organise.

'I've changed my mind,' he said. 'There are plenty of other companies I can sell these pieces to. Companies who take this more seriously than—'

The phone vibrated again, interrupting him in mid-flight, and this time Lark made a sound. Her gaze darted to the phone on the table.

'Are you listening?' He knew he sounded demanding and graceless, but he'd come to the end of his patience and once that occurred, he was done. 'Because if you're not—'

'I'm so sorry,' Lark said quickly as the phone vibrated again. 'But I really need to get this. It's my daughter's nanny. This is the first time I've left Maya for longer than a day since she was born and well…' She broke off as the phone vibrated yet again, her attention on the screen. 'Sorry, I just have to…' Before he could protest, she bent to pick the phone up off the table, turning as she looked down at it, presumably to hide whatever text she'd received.

She wasn't very tall, though, so he could see the screen over her shoulder. On it was a photo of a very young child, a little girl dressed in a pink nightgown and smiling at the camera. She had a cloud of soft rose-gold curls and blue, blue eyes.

It was a singular colour that rose gold, as was the intense blue of her eyes. He'd never met anyone else who'd had hair that hue apart from his mother. And as for that blue…

That was Donati blue. Two hundred years ago the Donatis had been patrons of a painter who'd created a paint colour in their honour. And that's what he'd called it.

It was famous.

Cesare went very still as everything in him slowed down and stopped. Everything except his brain, which was now working overtime. Going back over dates. Going back over that night. Going over everything.

Because if there was one thing he knew, it was that the little girl in that photo was his daughter.

CHAPTER TWO

LARK IMMEDIATELY RELAXED at the sight of Maya's smile on her screen. It was fine; of course it was fine. Emily had only sent her a happy photo, making it clear that Maya was feeling better.

Lark's central nervous system could stand down. Everything was okay.

Completely forgetting that she'd just broken off in midconversation, she began to type a reply, only for a large male hand to reach over her shoulder and pluck the phone from her grasp.

She gasped and turned round sharply to find Signor Donati staring down at her phone's screen, the expression on his handsome face almost frightening in its intensity.

Lark's stomach tightened. Why had he grabbed her phone? And why was he looking at the picture of Maya as if he was…angry? She should have been paying attention, she knew that, and answering texts in the middle of a professional conversation was very rude. But it was her daughter. Surely he'd understand?

She plastered a smile on her face. 'I'm so sorry about that text, but—'

'This is your daughter?' He looked up from the phone,

the blue of his eyes piercing her right through, the expression in them stealing her breath.

She didn't want to answer, an inexplicable unease sitting deep in her gut. Yet she couldn't think of a good reason not to. 'Yes,' she said slowly. 'That's Maya.'

He glanced back at the photo. 'Maya,' he repeated, his accent making her name sound like music.

Lark swallowed, her unease deepening. 'Can I have my phone back, please?'

He ignored her. 'When was she born?'

The uneasiness turned over inside her. Why was he asking her questions about her child? She didn't like it. She didn't like it at all.

'She just turned one a few months ago,' she said. 'I'm sorry, but why are you asking so many questions about—'

'And her father?'

Anger, heavy and unfamiliar, stirred to life in her gut. She tried never to get angry, it was such a depressing, useless emotion, but strange men asking her questions—deeply personal questions—about her and her daughter was a subject that she had no humour about.

'What about her father?' She kept her tone polite, because he was still a potential client, no matter his strange behaviour. 'I'm sorry, but I don't see how that is any of your—'

'Her father.' He looked up from the phone, his gaze all sharp blue edges. 'Who is he?'

He expected her to answer instantly, she could see that, and her usual reaction would be to soothe whatever was bothering him, because something clearly was. You caught more flies with honey than you did with vinegar, and Lark was an expert with honey.

But his line of questioning was deeply disquieting, not to mention that something about him had worked its way under her skin. His male beauty, the force of his presence, the air of authority that cloaked him, the way her heart suddenly seemed to beat out of rhythm when she looked at him… She wasn't sure which it was. Maybe all three. Whatever the reason, she didn't want to soothe him. Didn't want to give him her smile, smooth over all those sharp edges. So she didn't.

She gave him a cool look instead and said, still polite, 'I'm very sorry, but as I said, that's none of your business. I'm here to talk about the antiques you want to sell, not my daughter.'

His perfect features had hardened and the knuckles of his long-fingered hands were white where they held her phone. His gaze glittered and she was sure it was fury she saw there. He looked…dangerous and she was conscious that they were in the room together, alone. And he was a stranger, tall and powerful and so much bigger than she was. It wasn't that she was afraid of him exactly—or at least it wasn't *only* fear that wound through her. There was something else, something hotter…

'You don't remember me, do you?' he said.

Lark took a breath, her disquiet turning into a kernel of ice sitting in her gut.

No. It couldn't be. It couldn't…

'Should I remember you?' she asked carefully. 'I think I'd remember if we met.'

'We did meet,' he said. 'One night in Rome. You had your handbag stolen.'

The ice inside her froze her all the way through.

That night in Rome, the night she'd lost all memory of. The night she'd chosen to view through rose-coloured glasses because it had given her Maya. She'd thought she'd worked through all her fears about it, how her pregnancy could have been the result of rape or some kind of coercion, because she'd never had much to do with men and that was by choice. And after she'd seen the psychologist, she'd made a conscious decision not to keep revisiting that night, because how she'd got pregnant wasn't as important as its eventual outcome: Maya.

Her daughter was the most important person in Lark's life and she was all that mattered. Lark had told herself that it was even a good thing she didn't remember, because then it meant she didn't have to track down Maya's father and inform him of what had happened. She didn't have to deal with him or any demands he might make, and having witnessed that with her mother, it wasn't an experience she'd ever wanted for herself or for any children she might have.

It did mean that Maya wouldn't ever have a father figure in her life, but that wasn't a problem. Lark had never had one herself and her life had been all the better for it.

Except now Signor Donati was staring at her with sharp blue eyes, the force of his attention, the fury in it, almost a physical weight crushing her, and she was basically made of icy shock.

'No,' she said, her voice a tiny bit hoarse. 'I…don't remember.'

He didn't move and he didn't look away. 'I organised a new passport for you and then I took you out for dinner. We talked until the restaurant closed and then I invited you back to my villa. You said yes.'

Her mouth dried, the beat of her heart even louder in her ears. 'I… I…'

'We had some very good cognac in my library,' he went on relentlessly. 'And around midnight, we decided to move our conversation to my bedroom.'

No, it couldn't have been him. It *couldn't*. She would have remembered *him*.

'I told you that one night was all we could have and you agreed. I left you sleeping the next morning, and when I returned home, you'd gone.'

Lark shook her head, the cold shock making her extremities feel numb. She *did* remember her handbag being stolen and she'd been very upset about it. In fact, her last memory of that night was standing in a Roman street, wondering what on earth she was going to do, and then…nothing. Nothing until she'd opened her eyes and found herself in hospital.

Surely—*surely*—she would have remembered spending the night with him.

'I don't think that's what happened,' she said, her voice sounding thin. 'I'm sure I—'

'That's exactly what happened.' His gaze bored into hers. 'Why are you pretending you don't remember? Did you not want me to find out that I had a child?'

She blinked, the shock intensifying. 'No, of course not. And I'm not—'

'She has rose-gold hair.' He took a step towards her, still holding on to her phone, his gaze like a knife. 'My mother had hair like that, it's not a common colour. And no one but Donatis have eyes that blue.'

Lark couldn't help darting a glance at the portrait above the fire, at the woman sitting in the chair. Was that his mother? Because her hair was that colour and yes, if you looked at it in a certain light, it *was* the same colour as Maya's. And the man standing beside her with the blue eyes… The same blue as the eyes of the man standing in front of her.

Maya's eyes.

'Do you want money?' His voice was hard and cold and furious. 'Is that why you're here? Do you want to blackmail me?' He took a step closer and she found herself backing away. 'Did you do it on purpose? Are you planning to use your child to extort money out of me?'

The couch pressed against the backs of her legs, stopping her from going any further, and he was very close, towering over her, all six foot three of masculine fury. She could feel his heat, smell his aftershave, something warm and woody, like a cedar forest. And again she felt that tug inside her, her skin tightening. Not fear, and yet not unlike it. Anticipation, maybe or excitement, as if she relished that fury of his and wanted to see more of it. Which was crazy, because who wanted to see more masculine anger?

Also, how dare he shout at her? How dare he fling these questions at her, giving her no time to answer or think about what he was saying? And more than anything else, how dare he physically intimidate her in this way?

Lark never got angry and she never shouted. She tried to keep a positive outlook on everything she did. Years on the run from Lark's father had made her mother fragile and easily prone to depression, and God knew her mother didn't need Lark being difficult. She'd wanted her mother to be happy and her mother was only happy when Lark was. So she made sure to always be happy. Always be cheerful and optimistic, with never a bad word for anyone, and it hadn't been hard. Her mother had loved her for it.

So she had no idea where the hot anger that flooded her veins now had come from, or why. Because anger would only make this situation worse. She should be smiling at Signor Donati, soothing him somehow, or charming him out of his rage instead.

Yet she didn't do any of those things. She'd been worried about Maya and nervous about what Mr Ravenswood had expected of her, and then this horrible man had started throwing questions like daggers at her about a particularly sensitive time in her life, so now she had no interest in soothing him. And apart from anything else, anger was infinitely preferable to the cold fear that was now working its way through her.

So she lifted her chin and glared at him. 'Get out of my space,' she said angrily, and without waiting for him to move, she lifted her hands to his chest to push him away.

And froze.

He was very warm, the muscles beneath the wool of his suit jacket hard. That scent of his kept tugging at her, making her breathless. Making her skin prickle and tighten, as if her body knew something or remembered something she didn't.

He was looking down at her and there was something hot in his eyes now, a steady, hungry, blue flame and it mesmerised her. Her breath caught.

Men had never been a priority, not even as a teenager. Her mother had made her all too aware of how men could use you, trap you, hurt you if you weren't careful, so she'd always been careful. Which was why her pregnancy had come as such a shock and why she'd been glad that the accident had taken her memory.

So, she hadn't been expecting her own physical response to Cesare Donati, not the moment he'd walked into the room, and definitely not now. When she'd wanted to push him away and instead found her hands lingering on his chest, unable to tear her gaze from the hungry glitter in his eyes.

And when he said softly, 'Perhaps you'll remember this then,' and put a finger underneath her chin, tipping her head back, she didn't protest. And when he lowered his head and brushed his mouth over hers, she didn't avoid it.

Time seemed to stop, her world narrowing to this moment.

His kiss was unexpectedly light, unexpectedly gentle, his lips much softer than she'd thought they'd be. The touch of them on hers was electric, a bolt of white-hot sensation arrowing straight through her. Her nipples hardened against the lace of her bra, a pressure gathering between her thighs.

Sometimes at night she'd wake up aching, her skin sensitised, her head full of dreams of being touched and caressed. Of warm fingers stroking her, of a mouth on hers, of deep physical pleasure. She'd never understood where those dreams had come from and had never connected them with that night she'd forgotten.

But now…it was almost as if the memory was there.

As if she could reach out and grab it. As if she even wanted to…

If he's Maya's father, he'll take her away from you and you know it.

The wave of cold fear swamped her, drowning the effects of the kiss and she pushed at him, hard.

He didn't resist, going back a couple of steps, his broad chest rising and falling rapidly. His eyes glittered. 'You do remember,' he said, his accent much thicker. 'You do.'

'No.' She tried to still the shaking in her hands. 'I don't. I don't remember anything about you. Yes, I was in Rome and yes, I remember my handbag being stolen. But that's all.' She took an uneven breath. 'I was in an accident. I was knocked over by a car in the street and the next thing I remember is waking up in hospital. My memory of that night is gone.'

His gaze narrowed. 'An accident?'

'I was concussed. They told me that my memory of that night would return, but it never did.' She swallowed. 'I'm telling you the truth, Mr Donati. I have no memory of that night. But one thing I do know is that Maya is not yours.'

She couldn't be. She absolutely couldn't. Maya was no one's but hers.

He took no notice, the focused look in his eyes unchanging. 'I'm afraid I must insist on a paternity test.'

'No,' she said before she could stop herself. 'I won't allow it.'

His jaw tightened. 'If you know for certain that your daughter isn't mine, then a paternity test wouldn't matter would it?'

Lark felt her face get hot, her anger mounting. 'She's *not* yours. And I won't have my daughter's privacy invaded.'

'I see.' He drew himself up to his full height, authority radiating from him. 'If that's how you want to play it then fine. But if you won't allow a paternity test then I'm afraid I'll be taking my priceless Renaissance antiques elsewhere.'

Her anger became outrage and she knew it was a mistake to give in to it. That she should be smiling and giving him what he wanted instead, because everything was always easier that way. There was never any point in being difficult.

But he'd casually upended her nice, safe little world, first with his claims of being Maya's father and then with that kiss. Now there was a part of her that was afraid. Afraid that he was right, that she had in fact slept with him, and her daughter was his. And that he'd take Maya from her the way her father had tried to take her from her mother.

Men did that, didn't they? They took what they viewed as theirs, including people. And if they didn't take, then they threatened, which was exactly what he was doing now.

Mr Ravenswood would be very upset with her at losing the Donatis as clients, but her daughter was far more important than any antique. Her daughter was priceless and Lark would fight anyone who dared to take Maya from her. She'd fight them to the death if need be.

'Fine,' she snapped before she could think better of it.

'Take them elsewhere. Because you will not be testing my daughter. Not today, not tomorrow, not ever.'

Cesare was utterly furious, yet he found himself almost admiring the way Lark Edwards stood there, with her pointed chin lifted, determination in every line of her small, curvy figure.

No one had stood up to him like this in a very long time and he had to respect the courage it must have taken her to do so. He was, after all, one of the richest and most important men in Europe and everyone did what he told them to. They certainly didn't argue with him the way she was doing right now, and most especially not when he was angry.

And he *was* angry. That little girl on her phone *was* his, he knew it in his bones, though he'd had no idea how it had happened. He'd always been meticulous when it came to protection and that night had been no different. She'd told him she was on the pill too. Nothing had been left to chance.

So there shouldn't have been a pregnancy at all and yet there was no denying the colour of the little one's hair or the blue of her eyes. No denying the instinct that had gripped him, the knowledge that had settled inside him as hard and sure as the earth beneath his feet.

Maya was his daughter. And that meant he had some decisions to make.

It would be easy to agree with Lark, to accept that indeed he wasn't her father, that he couldn't be. To let Lark look at these antiques, take her pictures, and then leave Italy. He'd never have to see her again, never have to think about her again, and certainly never have to accept that he even had a daughter.

Yet he'd seen that photo now and he knew he was no longer the only Donati left, that there was another. Nothing could erase that knowledge, nothing could change it. The Donati line *would* continue, whether he wanted it to or not, and so he had to alter his course of action.

He could never forget what his parents had done to him, how their petty jealousies and pointless grudges, their burning, relentless hatred of each other, had killed them both and nearly ended him. And he'd never wanted to repeat that cycle. Never wanted a family where that might happen.

But now Maya existed, and because she existed, the cycle could repeat itself. And he was almost certain it would. The Donatis were hot-headed grudge holders, not to mention rigid and dictatorial, and compromise had never been in their vocabulary. Their selfishness was innate, he was positive, and Maya had the potential to be the same.

He couldn't let her. He had to take charge, teach her how to manage the Donati flaws, help her grow up to be a better person, a better person than he was. A better person than either of his parents.

He also had the opportunity to create something new out of the ashes of the old, something different. Something new. A legacy without all the emotional manipulation his parents used, lashing out at each other and using their child as a go-between. A legacy without hatred or rage. Where a child was safe.

In fact, the more he thought about it, the more certain he became. Under his guidance, Maya could be part of a new generation, the start of a healthier legacy that would erase the toxic history of his family.

There was, of course, one small catch. Lark.

She was standing in front of him, that gorgeous smile of hers gone. Her face was pink with anger, her sea-green eyes fierce and determined.

Kissing her had been a mistake and he knew it. He'd hoped it would remind her of their physical chemistry that night, jolt her into admitting she'd been pretending all along. Yet it had backfired on him, reminding him of how good it had been to have her beneath him, and he didn't need any more memories of that. Especially considering she'd said that she had none.

An accident that had erased her memory…

He wasn't sure he believed her. It seemed far-fetched and a little too convenient, and made him wonder if she was lying in order to keep her child. He couldn't blame her for that. He might even do the same thing himself, though it wouldn't make any difference.

Maya was his and now he knew about her, now he'd made the decision to claim her, he was going to do so immediately and nothing and no one was going to stand in his way. He hadn't let anyone do so before and he wouldn't let anyone do so now.

Only your parents.

Ah, but that was different. He'd only been a boy back then, thinking that if he was obedient enough, good enough, they wouldn't argue about him any more. That they wouldn't argue, full stop. It had all been in vain, though. Nothing had made them stop hurting each other and him, and after they'd died, after his mother had nearly killed him, the only thing he could think was that if you couldn't beat them, you joined them.

So he had. People did what he said, jumped through his hoops, or simply jumped when he told them to because that's what he wanted and what he wanted he got.

He was a Donati through and through, and Donatis were selfish, and he didn't care.

'If you don't want a paternity test, then you don't want one,' he said. 'But I'm claiming my daughter regardless.'

A hot green spark lit in her eyes and perhaps it was perverse of him to enjoy that spark even more than her bright, placating smile. Nevertheless, he did. He liked the angry flush in her cheeks too. That same flush had been there the night he'd lain between her thighs and pleasured her with his tongue, leaving her trembling and crying out his name.

'You will not,' she said hotly. 'She's not yours. She's no one's but mine.'

'Do you really think you can stop me, Miss Edwards? I have governments in my pocket and resources you can't possibly imagine. If I want her, I'll take her and there's nothing you can do about it.'

He expected her to give in. That she'd realise how little power she had in this scenario and that giving him exactly what he wanted was the best course of action.

Except she didn't.

Instead she took a step forward, getting into his personal space in much the same way as he'd got into hers. As if she wasn't afraid of him or the fact that he was nearly a full foot taller than she was.

She looked up into his face, her eyes full of fury, and

a very male part of him growled in appreciation. She was *exceptionally* pretty when she was angry.

'That's really how you want to play this?' she demanded. 'You'd take my daughter away from her home? Rip her away from everything she's ever known, including her mother just because you feel some kind of strange territorial possessiveness?'

He stiffened at her tone. 'That's not what—'

'How dare you?' She took another step, her eyes blazing. 'How *dare* you think you can take my daughter from me? Men like you are all the same. Just because you're rich and powerful, you think that can take whatever you want.' She took yet another step closer, and this time, rather to his own surprise, he found he was the one taking an automatic step back. 'She's only a little over a year old,' Lark continued fiercely. 'She's a *baby.* Don't you care how that might affect her?' She stepped forward again and again he stepped back. 'But no, you don't care, do you? You don't care about how that might affect her or me. And God, you *kissed* me, damn you.' She continued forward, her hands clenched into fists at her side, her green eyes glittering with outrage. 'Did you ever think that perhaps that wouldn't be welcome? That I might not want it? No, of course you didn't. It never occurred to you because the only thing you care about is yourself, you stupid, selfish, *horrible* man!'

Cesare found himself backed halfway to the doorway, Lark standing furiously in front of him, her delicate features pink, her eyes full of fire. And he was glad she didn't actually have a weapon in her possession, because he was pretty sure she might have used it on him.

He was surprised she hadn't lashed out with one of those small, tightly clenched fists.

And while some of him was incensed that she'd had the gall to speak to him like that, most of him was shocked. Because no one *did* speak to him like that, let alone a woman he barely knew.

Are you surprised? You told her you were going to take her child from her.

Fine. Maybe he'd been hasty with that threat. Maybe he'd let his anger at the situation run away with him, which was *always* a mistake. The hot Donati temper was a flaw he had to keep in check, and he'd always prided himself on his control over his emotions. Clearly, though, in this instance, his control wasn't as good as he'd thought. He didn't give other people's feelings much thought either, but he had to admit that the fury in Lark's eyes got to him.

In fact, now that he thought about it, taking his daughter the way he'd threatened to wasn't the change he'd been hoping to make. Giovanni had taken *him* away from Bianca, his mother, and he knew how that had ended. He couldn't do the same thing, especially when he was hoping to start a new legacy.

Yes, he was a selfish man and he owned that. He was exactly as his parents had made him. But he didn't want that for the next generation, which meant he needed to set a better example. Start as he meant to continue and all that.

Cesare was used to changing his mind quickly. Being adaptable was vital in business, because rigidity meant stagnation and that's all the Donatis had been doing for centuries. Doing the same thing, going over the same ground. Wasting time killing the competition because that was 'the Donati way' instead of changing how they dealt with that competition.

He had to change now. Because while all the accusations Lark had thrown at him were correct, there was one that wasn't. He might be selfish and horrible, but he wasn't stupid.

Gritting his teeth, he put a leash on his temper and looked down at her, standing so small and indomitable in front of him. A wisp of golden hair had come out of her ponytail and lay across one pink cheekbone.

She was as lovely as he remembered, all soft and sweet and smelling of vanilla. He could still feel the brush of her mouth against his from that ill-advised kiss…

'You're entitled to your opinion of me, little bird.' He injected as much cool into his tone as he could to drain the heat from the moment. 'Some of it may even be correct. However, I'm nothing if not an excellent businessman and so I'll offer you a deal. You allow me a paternity test and if your daughter isn't mine, you'll never hear from me again. And if she is, then we'll sit down like civilised human beings and decide what to do from there.'

CHAPTER THREE

LARK WAS PRACTICALLY vibrating with rage, even as a part of her was appalled at how completely she'd lost her head. Calling him a horrible, selfish man was way out of line, especially when he was not only a stranger to her, but also a potential and very important client for Ravenswood Antiques.

Except not only had he brought up what had been a terrifying time in her life, that she'd thought she'd put behind her, he'd also gone after the one thing she'd do anything to protect: Maya. He'd threatened to take her daughter and she wasn't going to stand for it.

When her father had threatened to take Lark away from her mother, Grace Edwards's answer had been to run, and that had been fair since her father had been powerful and had money, while her mother had nothing. She'd taken Lark out of France, where she'd been born, and escaped to Australia, Grace's home country, where she'd managed to keep Lark hidden away for years.

Lark didn't know anything about Cesare Donati himself, but his family's history made it clear that they were ruthless and let nothing stand in their way when it came to getting what they wanted. He would come after her, she was sure of it, and then she'd be forced into the same situation as her mother had been. Grace had done what she could for Lark, but being on the run continually hadn't made for a great childhood, and God knew, Lark didn't want that for Maya.

Signor Donati had folded his arms across his broad chest and was looking down at her from his great height, his blue eyes now as cool as the ice in his voice. He was so much taller and more powerful than she was, and not only physically. Yet he'd still let himself be backed halfway across the room by her. And yes, he'd definitely *let* her.

She didn't know how to feel about that, whether to be pleased that she'd managed to unsettle him, or to be even more furious at being placated. But while she couldn't deny that allowing herself to be angry with him had felt oddly freeing, she couldn't permit herself any more. That really *would* be a mistake. She'd already called him a stupid, selfish, horrible man and that would disappoint Mr Ravenswood.

'Well?' Signor Donati demanded, impatience in his deep voice.

She tried to get a handle on her anger, forcing herself to put it aside and think objectively about the deal he'd offered.

He could be lying about being Maya's father; that was the issue, though, why he'd lie about it she had no idea. Also, he wasn't wrong. A paternity test *would* clear up that side of things. Certainly if Maya ended up *not* being his then Lark wouldn't have to deal with him again.

And if she is *his?*

He'd promised they'd sit down like civilised adults and talk, so that was something. Still, she didn't want to even think about that possibility yet, and she wasn't going to allow any testing to happen until she had that promise in writing. She wouldn't allow Mr Ravenswood to be penalised either.

'Okay,' she said. 'But I want you to promise that you'll also sell your antiques to Ravenswood. If you take your business elsewhere, Mr Ravenswood would be very disappointed, and this situation has nothing to do with him. It's between us.'

His gaze narrowed to sharp splinters of blue and he was silent a long moment. Then he said, 'I will not be apologising for that kiss.'

A sparking, prickling electricity shivered over her skin as the memory of his lips on hers stole through her, making her face feel hot yet again, and a thread of anger escaped. 'Like hell you won't,' she said flatly. 'You took it without asking and I'll be having that apology, in addition to all those other promises, in writing.'

A muscle in his jaw ticked. 'You don't trust my word?'

'No. I wouldn't trust you as far as I could throw you.'

He tilted his head, heat flickering in his eyes again. 'You did that night. You trusted me enough to come to my bed.'

The prickle of electricity over Lark's skin became more intense, a throbbing ache she'd never felt before gripping her. 'Do you have to mention that?' she asked tightly.

His hard mouth curved. 'It seems relevant to the situation at hand.'

Don't you wish you could remember, though? What it must have been like to sleep with him?

No. No she didn't wish it. She was glad, very glad,

that she didn't remember. In fact, she'd come to a place of peace with it, and she would have been quite happy for those memories never to return, except...

There was a rising heat inside her, and she couldn't help but notice how his suit jacket seemed to highlight the impressive width of his shoulders, while his trousers did wonderful things to his lean waist and powerful thighs. He wore a plain white business shirt and a silk tie that echoed the deep blue of his eyes, and he...

Her mouth dried. He was just beautiful.

'You were willing,' he went on, his voice softer, deeper. 'Very willing, in fact. Which also seems relevant.'

Unexpectedly, something tight and hard inside her that she'd thought she'd put behind her after Maya had been born, relaxed. The sessions she'd had with the psychologist had helped with her fears around that night, but there had always been a little splinter of uncertainty she'd never been able to get rid of.

You weren't raped or forced. That's something.

Perhaps. If she believed him.

'I only have your word for that,' she said, not wanting to admit anything to him just yet.

His imperious dark brows rose. 'You really think I'd take an unwilling woman to bed?'

'I don't know,' she said. 'Would you?'

'Absolutely not,' he replied, with no hesitation at all. 'Why would I? When I have an embarrassment of willing women to choose from?'

You're not making things better.

Lark took a deep, silent breath. No, she wasn't. And

throwing around accusations of sexual assault wouldn't help the situation.

Yet even though her shock was wearing off a little, that kernel of ice was still sitting in the pit of her stomach. Him telling her that she'd spent the night with him hadn't jogged anything loose. Not even that kiss had. She also found it difficult to believe that he'd wanted her. Because why? She was a nobody, and while she might be inoffensive to look at, she certainly wasn't in supermodel territory. She didn't have much idea about what kind of women men like him went for, but she was pretty certain it wasn't women like her.

'Why me, then?' she asked, since as he'd said, that 'seemed relevant'.

The look in his eyes gleamed. 'Why do you want to know? Do you want to remember?'

She felt herself flushing yet again. She *didn't* want to know. She *didn't* want to remember. She'd put her fears and doubts about that night into a box and shoved them into a corner of her mind, never to be opened again.

Yet now Signor Donati, damn him, had opened that box and all those fears and doubts were spilling out again. What if that night had been terrible, for example? What if the conception of her beautiful daughter had been hurried, awkward and unpleasant? What if the man she'd slept with had been a liar? What if he'd been drunk? What if he'd been married? What if he'd slipped something into her drink and she had no injuries because she'd been unconscious?

What if he is *telling the truth? What if you* did *sleep with him? And what if that night was good?*

Yet even admitting that possibility felt dangerous,

since she didn't understand how she'd ever have agreed to go to dinner with him, let alone go back to his villa, no matter how helpful or attractive she'd found him. She simply didn't trust men enough for that, and especially not a powerful man like this one.

So no, she didn't know why she was asking him about that night. She wasn't curious and she didn't need to know, because there was going to be no interaction between them after this.

That paternity test would prove that he wasn't Maya's father.

Why are you so sure about that?

Because she wouldn't accept any other outcome.

'No,' she said shortly. 'I don't want to know. Forget I ever said anything.'

His blue gaze never left hers and he studied her for another long moment. Then he said unexpectedly, 'I did not hurt you. And you should know that you wanted me every bit as badly as I wanted you.'

Lark's heartbeat thumped. She couldn't imagine wanting any man badly, let alone this one, not when he was everything she should hate. How had it happened? How had she managed to get herself seduced—

No, she didn't want to know. She didn't want to fall into an endless doubt spiral about what had happened that night, where there were too many questions and not enough answers.

Cesare Donati might have the answers you're looking for.

He might. But he could also be lying and as she'd already told him, she didn't trust him. Not an inch. All those stories about him that she'd read on the plane had mentioned his many lovers, and while he was supposedly childless, for all she knew he not only had a woman in every port, but a couple of unacknowledged bastards too. He was also reputed to treat his lovers well—who really knew? He could be abusive and paying people to stay quiet.

'Sorry,' she said, steeling herself. 'But I don't believe you. And as to the rest of your promises, like I said, I'm going to need them and that apology, in writing.'

He eyed her. 'I would not lie to you. Not about that night.'

'I don't care. If I don't have your signature on a piece of paper agreeing to all those things you just said, then you're not going to see Maya.'

His expression tightened a moment, then it smoothed and he shrugged as if none of this was of any moment. 'Very well. I will have my legal team draw up something for you.'

Lark, expecting him to keep arguing, gave him a suspicious look. Had she missed something? Was there a catch somewhere perhaps?

You catch more flies with honey, don't forget.

Oh, she couldn't forget. She had to stay calm, stay polite. Bury her outrage. However, she wasn't going to let him get away with dictating everything. He might have all the money and all the power, but she was Maya's mother. And if he wanted access, then he'd have to go through Lark to get it.

'Thank you.' She kept her voice cool.

'So, how long are you here?'

'Just tonight. I'll be flying back to London tomorrow. I want to get back to Maya as soon as I can.'

'Of course, you do,' he said. 'Would you prefer to leave tonight?'

Her gaze narrowed. Why was he being so agreeable now? 'I would, yes,' she said. 'But there were no flights available tonight and I wasn't sure how long it would take being here.'

'It will take no time at all,' he said smoothly. 'What time would you like to fly home?'

She stared at him, taken aback. 'All the flights were full. At least they were when I last checked.'

'They are not full.' There was nothing but supreme confidence in his voice. 'My jet can accommodate you.'

Lark blinked. 'Your what?'

'My private jet. It can leave whenever we're ready.'

'Wait.' Her gut tightened. 'What do you mean 'we'?'

His eyes gleamed, hot and blue. 'I mean, I'll be coming with you.'

'No,' Lark said, anger once more leaping in her eyes. 'You absolutely will not.'

He'd been expecting her to say that, but unfortunately, he wasn't going to give her any choice. He'd be coming to London with or without her, because now that she'd agreed to his deal—and he was glad she had—he'd decided that he wanted to see his daughter ASAP.

'Fine,' he said easily. 'Then I'll take my jet and you can fly commercial. I hope you can find a flight tonight, but if not, we can meet tomorrow in London.'

Her chin jutted, her expression tightening with frustration. 'Why do you want to come to London at all?'

He shouldn't feel pleased that he was getting to her or satisfied, because really, who was she to him? A one-night stand two years ago, that was all. Yet, he couldn't deny that he was relishing the anger in her lovely eyes and the stain of pink in her pretty skin. And the primitive male part of him wanted to keep pushing her, find out exactly how much she remembered of the night they'd spent together. Because he was sure that even if the injury had wiped her memory, her body hadn't forgotten him.

Her mouth had been soft under his when he'd kissed her, her hands on his chest exerting no pressure. She hadn't avoided his kiss and the pulse at the base of her throat had been beating hard and fast. Her pupils had been dilated as he'd raised his head, and he was sure the flush in her cheeks hadn't been anger then.

Until she'd pushed him away, of course, which she'd had every right to do.

Still, her body remembered and he was tempted, so tempted, to test that. Then again, she'd had to push him away because he'd forgotten himself and if one kiss had the power to do that to him, then testing her might very well test him, and he couldn't afford that. Not again. That night had been a one-off and he hadn't changed his mind.

In fact, perhaps it was even a blessing that she didn't remember. That way he didn't need to fight his own urge to revisit it as well as hers, since obviously if she had remembered, she'd want another night. They all did.

So there would be no more kisses, and whatever chemistry was between them, he'd let it lie. He didn't need to revisit that particular memory and he wasn't going to.

'Obviously I need to speak with Mr Ravenswood personally,' he said. 'And the sooner the better. I would also like to visit my daughter.'

Lark looked as if she wanted to shout at him again,

and it was probably wrong of him to hope that she might. She was like an angry kitten, all small and soft, turning her sharp claws on him, and part of him wanted to see what else she might do if he got her really wound up.

She hadn't been like that the night they'd had in Rome. She'd talked to him openly about her life and how much she'd loved her mother. There had been something about a custody battle with her French father, and how her mother had taken her away to bring her up in Australia. How they'd had to move around a lot in case anyone found them.

He'd been intrigued by the story and had empathised with her, making oblique references to his own struggles with his parents, though he hadn't told her the whole truth.

About how his mother had ultimately tried to kill him and then his father had shot her and then himself. That had been too dark a story and he hadn't wanted to go into it.

Lark had been so sympathetic and concerned at what he had told her. They'd been sitting in the library of his villa and she'd been leaning forward, listening. Then once he'd told her all about it, she'd put one small hand over his and that had been all it had taken for their steadily building chemistry to ignite.

Her touch had burned and when he'd looked into her eyes, he'd seen all that sea-green catch alight too, and when he'd pulled her into his arms, she hadn't resisted. Her mouth had been soft and hot, opening beneath his as if they were lovers already, and her arms had twined around his neck. She'd clung to him as if she hadn't been able to bear letting him go.

But he couldn't think about that night. It was over and done with.

'You can't see Maya,' Lark snapped. 'I forbid it.'

'Very well,' he replied smoothly. 'Then I'll wait until after the paternity test results come through.'

'You'll be waiting a while, so you won't need to come to London now, will you?'

'On the contrary. I can get test results the same day, and of course I'll need to meet with Ravenswood.'

She was breathing very fast, anger glittering in her eyes.

You are being unfair. She's Maya's mother and she's likely to be in shock. Why are you letting your wounded pride get to you?

The thought sent a sharp jolt through him. His pride wasn't wounded, of course it wasn't. And one woman not remembering their one-night stand didn't affect him in the slightest. His child was important and worth fighting for, that was all. It was true that if she'd indeed had an accident, then it wasn't her fault that she hadn't let him know about Maya's existence. It was also fair to say that since he was a complete stranger to her, him threatening to take her daughter must be frightening. Especially considering what she'd told him about her own father and how he'd pursued her and her mother.

It was clear she thought Cesare would do the same and doing nothing to dispel her doubts wasn't helping either of them.

Cesare had always been sure of himself and of what he wanted, and anger had propelled him to take charge of Donati Bank and institute all the changes his father had always refused to make, hauling a centuries-old bank into the twenty-first century.

He'd got rid of the accounts of tax evaders and money launderers, of arms dealers and drug barons, of dictators and terrorists. He made transparent secretive bank practices and opened special accounts for charities with excellent interest rates, zero fees and competitive financial management services.

Burning the old rules of his ancestors made Donati Bank *better.*

But anger wasn't his fuel any longer. Like love, it was a toxic emotion and one he'd put away. He still didn't much care for the emotions of others, though, and yet he was contemplating Lark's feelings now and it concerned him that he felt almost…guilty for threatening her. She was only defending her child and in her place he would have done the same. In fact, he'd probably have done worse.

'I just want to see her, little bird,' he said, softening his tone slightly. 'I'm not going to take her away from you.'

Lark's expression remained suspicious and angry. 'Why do you call me that?'

Something inside him jolted. He hadn't realised he'd even said it and now he had the impression that he'd said it more than once. 'I called you that in our night together,' he admitted reluctantly. 'You liked it.'

'Well, I don't now.' She eyed him. 'Nothing I say to you will make you change your mind will it?'

He was adaptable, it was true, but once a course of action had been decided on, he never changed it. Especially if he felt strongly about that course of action, and he did now.

'No,' he said. 'It will not.' He held her gaze, let her see the truth. Let her see the ruthlessness that made him a Donati of old through and through. He'd been brought up to be as terrible as his ancestors and he was. He made no apology for that.

But he would be the last of them.

Maya would be the first of a better, brighter generation. A kinder generation.

He'd make sure of it.

Lark took a breath and glanced away. Her hands uncurled from their fists, fingers stretching out a couple of times as if she was trying to relax them.

'Fine,' she said after a moment, looking back at him. 'But she'll be asleep when we get home and I'm not waking her up just so you can see her. You'll have to wait until tomorrow morning.'

'I can live with that,' he said.

It would do him no harm to wait, and there was no point antagonising her more than he had already. She *was* Maya's mother after all, and while his own had been a ridiculous excuse for one, it was obvious that Lark was a different kettle of fish. She was fierce and protective, which his own mother, too involved in her own petty jealousies and intrigues over his father, had never been. He approved. In fact, he'd already decided that she would have to be a part of Maya's life.

Is that really your decision to make?

Well, no, it was hers too. But he'd meant what he said when he'd told her that he wouldn't take Maya away from her—a child needed a loving mother and it was obvious that Lark was indeed loving.

However, he wouldn't allow himself to be cut out

of her life either. She was a Donati, heir to a vast fortune and the poisonous legacy that came with it, and she would need him to guide her around the pitfalls and traps that being a Donati entailed.

She would need him to set her on the right path, to ensure that the poison that infiltrated his entire family tree stopped with him. That she would never carry the same stain.

Lark was still looking deeply unhappy at the thought of him coming to London. Too bad. She would have to get used to the idea of him being in her life now, the two of them tied to a little girl neither of them had expected.

'I just don't understand why you want this,' Lark said unexpectedly. 'You never even knew of her existence until ten minutes ago and now suddenly you want to run a paternity test and come to London to see her. Threaten to take her away from me. Why? She's nothing to you.'

'She is not nothing to me,' he said. 'And we shared more than our bodies that night, Lark. You won't remember, but I did tell you that I never wanted children. Never wanted a family, not with a history as toxic as the Donatis' history is. But then I saw the photo of her on your phone and I knew she was mine.'

'What? Just like that?'

He saw no reason to deny it. 'Yes, just like that. Call it an instinct. But whatever it was, I know she's my daughter, which makes her my responsibility. And I'm not a man who walks away from his responsibilities.'

'You can walk away from this one, believe me. I won't mind if you do. In fact, I'd even prefer that you do.'

'No.' He put every ounce of authority into the word. 'I will not leave any child of mine without a father, especially not a Donati child. She'll be my heir and inherit a wealth and a legacy that are beyond your wildest dreams, little bird. And she'll need me to guide her in how to manage both.'

Lark's lovely mouth tightened. 'Do you know how unbelievably arrogant that sounds?'

He shrugged. He didn't much care how arrogant or otherwise people thought he was. Arrogance was part and parcel of the Donati way, and he was all that and more. Arrogant, and selfish, just as his parents had been. But what made him different was that he owned it. They never had.

'I don't care how it sounds,' Cesare said. 'As long as you know that I will be part of Maya's life whether you want me to be or not.'

'Only if you're really her father. I could have slept with other men that night, you don't know.'

He allowed himself a smile at that. 'You were in my bed all night, Lark. And we didn't sleep. So unless you have the ability to be in two places at once, I'm pretty sure that the only man you were with that night was me.'

'I could have had a boyfriend.'

'But you didn't. You told me so.'

'I might have lied.'

But he was tired of this conversation. Now that he'd made the decision to fly to London, he was impatient to be there. Impatient to see Maya. And he had to get his lawyers to draw up an agreement, then let his staff know he'd be taking the jet.

'You didn't lie.' He walked over to the table and placed her phone down on it, then took his own out of his pocket and glanced down at the screen. 'You were a virgin.'

'What?'

He glanced up at her shocked gaze. 'You told me you were a virgin and indeed you were. Now, are you coming with me to London or are you going back to your hotel?'

CHAPTER FOUR

LARK BADLY WANTED to tell Cesare Donati where he could put his stupid agreement.

He'd handed it to her the moment they'd got on his luxurious private plane—how he'd managed to have it drawn up in the time it took for them to go from his palazzo to the private airport where he kept the Donati jet she didn't know, but she'd spent all the taxi and taking off time going over it.

She wasn't a lawyer, but she'd had to deal with various legal documents while being Mr Ravenswood personal assistant, so it wasn't a difficult read. In fact it was unfortunately very clear. She almost wished it wasn't, just so she could keep on arguing about it with him.

She badly wanted to keep on arguing with him full stop.

Deciding to fly with him instead of flying commercial had been a mistake, but there had been no seats available on any flights to London out of Rome that night, and since she wasn't going to let him get to London ahead of her—she didn't want him seeing Maya without her present and given the arrogance of the man, that was something he might insist on to spite her—she hadn't had much option but to take up his offer of a flight.

Which meant that now she had to spend the next couple of hours in the company of the man who'd casually informed her that she'd been a virgin when they'd spent the night together. The night she had no memory of.

She'd had no idea what to say to that, not that he'd given her any time to respond since by then he'd taken his phone out of his pocket and had started arranging seemingly the entire world, leaving her to be carried along in his wake.

The next couple of hours had been spent fuming about his arrogance since that was easier than contemplating the ice that sat in her gut as they'd dropped by her hotel to pick up her stuff before carrying on to the airport.

Now she was sitting in one of the plush white leather seats of his private jet, trying to find her usual good humour and failing miserably.

She was furious and afraid, and she didn't know what to do with either of those emotions, since she'd always tried very hard not to dwell on negative feelings.

Anger was better than fear though, so she gripped hard to it, thinking about how he'd casually pointed out her virginity to her, as if that was something she'd forgotten too. Because no, of course, she hadn't forgotten. In fact, that was another thing she'd lost in the aftermath of that night, her first sexual experience. The memory of that was gone, there was no going back, and she didn't need him pointing that out to her.

Damn Cesare Donati. Damn him to hell.

Anger doesn't help, remember?

Yet knowing that didn't ease the hot, bright stinging emotion that sat inside her. When she'd been a child, her mother's fragility would sometimes weigh on her. The feeling of having to always be the one who was happy and strong, of never being allowed to be angry or sad in case that would push her mother into another downward spiral. As if she was the mother and her mother was the daughter who had to be protected and kept safe.

It had been hard at times, so she used to take herself off and bury her head in a book, a distraction from all that sharp-edged, hot emotion, and most of the time that had worked. The emotion usually faded.

But there were no books here and the thing currently making her angry was right in her face, pacing up and down the plane's small aisle as he talked on his phone in rapid, musical Italian.

He didn't seem to be a man who knew what stillness was, his presence a relentless kinetic energy that had her tensing in her seat every time he strode past.

She wished he'd sit down, because it was starting to get to her.

You like it. You find it attractive.

Lark gritted her teeth, trying to drag her attention back to the stupid agreement she'd insisted he draw up, but she kept getting distracted by him walking up and down, brushing past her in a delicious cloud of cedar and heat. Making her achingly aware of his physicality, of the way he moved, purposefully and with an athletic, masculine grace that made her pulse race.

Her gaze drifted from the words in front of her up to his tall figure coming to the end of the aisle and then pacing back.

Had he been like that in bed, when they'd slept together? Had he been this purposeful and powerful? Had she let it overwhelm her? Had she let him seduce her?

You'll never know now, will you?

She didn't understand why that made her ache with a hollow kind of loss.

Her mother had warned her about men and all the ways they could hurt a woman, about how they could take advantage and manipulate. Lark had to be careful, she said. They might seem nice on the outside, wine and dine you and make you feel like a princess. But only once they'd caught you would their true colours become apparent, and that's when it became dangerous.

Lark's father hadn't been abusive until about a year into their marriage and by then Grace had been living in a country where she didn't speak the language and had no friends. She'd been isolated, cut off from her support networks, and then Lark had been born, making it impossible for Grace to leave.

It was your fault, you know that right? If you hadn't been born—

Lark shoved that thought from her head. It was a negative, depressing one and she didn't want it there.

Regardless, she'd taken to heart her mother's lessons on men and she couldn't think how Cesare Donati, arrogance personified and red flags from here to Australia, had managed to get under her defences.

He'd told her that they'd talked and talked for a long time. About what though? She couldn't imagine talking to him about anything, let alone for hours and hours. Then letting him seduce her, take her virginity… What had she been thinking?

It was true that she'd gone to Rome because she'd been grieving her mother. She'd just moved to England and escaping into a book wasn't enough this time to keep the dark thoughts at bay. She'd needed to get out of the cold, wet grey London, and had settled on Rome. Bright and sunny, with lots of history. Perfect, she'd thought.

Men had been the very last thing on her mind.

The first few days had been great, wandering the ancient streets and sightseeing, but then she'd been in a tour group at the Colosseum and had seen a family talking excitedly together. The man had hoisted a little girl on his shoulders while his wife had smiled and said something that had made all three of them laugh.

For some reason that had made her ache. She'd never had that. Never been part of a family laughing and enjoying each other's company. It had only ever been her and her mother, and her mother's relentless anxiety. They'd never gone on holiday, never even had a fun day out, not when Grace was constantly worried about the risk of discovery. It had been a tough childhood in many ways, though even thinking about it in those terms made Lark feel disloyal.

Her mother wouldn't have even been in that position if she hadn't had Lark.

Lark had felt…lonely. Then she'd had her handbag stolen, which hadn't helped, and then…she remembered nothing after that until the hospital. But in that blank space between realising her handbag had gone and waking up in the hospital bed, she'd met him. And he'd helped her, taken her out for dinner, taken her back to his house, and they'd…slept together.

He strode past her once again, keeping up a stream of Italian, and she watched him despite herself. Tall, powerful, authoritative. In total command of himself and the rarefied world he inhabited. Who was he talking to now? The prime minister of some country? The CEO of a huge multinational? The ruler of a nation?

She knew nothing about him beyond what was in the media, but he knew something of her and perhaps more than something. What had they talked about together? What had she told him? How had they connected so strongly that she'd given him her body?

Lark shut her eyes and tried to force her thoughts away from him. Thinking about him would only bring back her own feelings of dread about what had happened that night. About all the questions she didn't have answers to. It would undo all the work she'd done with the psychologist and the peace she'd come to with her lack of memories, and she didn't want that.

She had to look forward not back; that's what she had to keep telling herself. No matter how attractive he was or the current of excitement that hummed just beneath her skin, the unfamiliar ache of craving a touch she didn't remember.

Finally, the stream of Italian ceased as he stopped in the middle of the aisle and put his phone away. Then he turned and paced back to where she sat, pausing beside her seat.

'You have finished reading?' he asked. 'Is it acceptable?'

She badly wished there had been something she could nitpick, but she hadn't been able to find a single thing. Everything he'd promised was in there, even the apology for the kiss.

'Yes,' she said with very bad grace.

Without a word, he produced a pen, made her sign it then signed it himself with a flourish. Then he picked up the paper and like magic a stewardess appeared, taking the document from his outstretched hand and disappearing up the front of the plane.

'Does that always happen?' Lark asked.

He'd taken his phone out again and was staring at the screen. 'Does what always happen?'

'Someone appears out of nowhere to do your bidding without you even asking?'

'Generally, yes.' He put his phone back in his pocket, stared down at her for a moment. Then much to her discomfort, he deposited himself in the seat directly opposite hers, stretching his long legs out in front of him. 'Is that supposed to be another comment on my arrogance?'

She needed to find her smile again, find the good humour and optimism that had helped her mother through so many tough times, because she didn't like this anger that sat like a burning coal inside her. It was as if he'd ignited a fire inside her that now refused to go out and nothing she could do would get rid of it.

'No, of course not.' She forced herself to smile. 'Please forget I said it.'

He stared at her silently, his blue gaze laser-like in its focus. 'You have a pretty smile, little bird,' he said after a moment. 'But I think I prefer your anger. That at least isn't fake.'

The coal inside her glowed hot and no matter how hard she tried to resist, she couldn't stop herself from snapping, 'It's not fake.'

'Yes, it is. You're very angry with me so why bother smiling?'

'Because I'm trying to be polite,' she said tightly.

He tilted his head, frowning. 'Why?'

'Well, aside from the fact that you're a complete stranger, you're also a potential client of Mr Ravenswood.' She was aware she was clutching the armrests of her seat far too hard, her knuckles white. 'Not to mention that you're also a very powerful—'

'Yes, yes, a banker, a Donati heir, etcetera,' he interrupted impatiently. 'But you didn't seem to find all those such an issue the night we spent together, so why are they now?'

'Because first you threatened to take my child from me and wouldn't take no for an answer,' she shot back. 'Then you told me casually that the night we slept together, the night I remember nothing about, I was a virgin.'

'Yes,' he said without a single shred of shame. 'What of it?'

Lark took her hands off the arms of her seat and leaned forward. 'You don't think that I might be angry about any of that? That my child means nothing to me? That I might be horrified at the thought of my first time being with a man I'm liking less and less with each passing second, and who doesn't seem to care that I have no memory of being with him? Of losing my virginity to him?'

He tilted his head, studying her, and she could hear the anger and the thread of fear in her voice ringing uncomfortably loud in the interior of the plane. It seemed to be even louder than the engines.

Shame gripped her. Giving in to her anger was a mistake, no matter how afraid she was. There had been that time when she'd been ten years old and they'd stayed a couple of months in some tiny town in South Australia.

She'd made a friend, the first one she'd had for years, and she'd been starting to think that maybe this time they might stay. That her father had stopped looking and finally they were safe.

Then something had happened to make her mother scared and she'd come home from school to find everything packed and Grace trying to get her into the car because they were leaving. She'd screamed at her mother then, an eruption of rage bursting out of her, that no she wasn't going and how could her mother do this to her when Lark finally had a best friend? She didn't want to go. She wanted to stay there.

Grace hadn't got angry. She hadn't screamed back. No, what she'd done then had been worse. She'd burst into tears, sobbing and sobbing, making Lark feel like the worst person in the world.

'Please, Lark. I'm just trying to protect you,' Grace had wept. 'I'm just trying to keep us both safe. Don't you want us to be safe?'

Of course she did. And things were already hard. She didn't need to make them worse by upsetting her mother even more than she already had. So she'd swallowed her anger, done what Grace had asked and got into the car, and they'd left that small town, her mother silently crying all the way.

Anger hurt people. Yet Cesare Donati didn't look hurt or upset, or even annoyed. He just sat there looking smug, as if her anger hadn't touched him, and she had to admit that saying all those things to him in a fury had definitely felt…freeing.

'If you're waiting for me to apologise for that,' she said stiffly. 'You'll be waiting a long time.'

Signor Donati's blue gaze had become smoky, glittering as he studied her. 'Apologise for what?' His voice was deep and dark. 'You can say anything you like to me.' He was looking at her now as if he was hungry, as if she was a meal set before him and he was starving. 'You're pretty when you smile, little bird, but I think you're beautiful when you're angry.'

The excitement humming just beneath her skin crackled, her heart squeezing in her chest. No one had ever called her beautiful before and definitely not after she'd shouted in a temper.

'Don't say that,' she said huskily.

'Why shouldn't I? It's true. And all those things you said were true too. You have every right to be upset about your child, and as for your virginity… Well.' His gaze roamed over her as if he couldn't get enough of the sight of her. 'Let's just say you gave me a precious gift and I treated it as such.'

Her mouth was dry, her pulse still racing. 'I already told you, I only have your word for that.'

'And I am a man of my word.' One dark brow rose. 'If you doubt me, perhaps you need another reminder.'

The hot coal inside her flared, a burning ember, and this time she didn't know whether it was anger or something else, something hotter, something that matched the hunger in his eyes. Making her feel restless, making her ache.

He was turning her inside out, damn him. Making her feel as if she was a different person, someone angry and snappy and shrill. And no matter how freeing that might feel, she didn't like it.

'No, thank you.' She tried very hard to ignore that hot coal. 'I'm certain once was enough.'

Signor Donati said nothing, but his mouth curved and she found herself staring at the perfectly carved, full shape of his lower lip, the only thing that was soft about him. Everywhere else he seemed…hard. Certainly his chest had been hard when she'd reached up to push him, the muscles beneath the wool of his jacket like iron.

And that smile… There was a sensuality to it, a heat. A knowledge that taunted her, tugged at her. A knowledge echoed in the wicked glint of his blue eyes.

Her breath caught.

He was so devastatingly attractive and at the same time so completely smug, it was enraging.

He knows and you don't, so why continue to let him have that power?

A very good question. She'd been telling herself for two years she didn't want to know what had happened that night. She had Maya and she had to look to the future, not keep going over the past. But now Cesare Donati had come into her life and had casually upended it, and now she was questioning everything.

She didn't like his certainty or how he had this knowledge of her that she didn't herself. It made her feel vulnerable, and she didn't want to feel vulnerable, not around a man like him.

She was also tired of not knowing. Tired of questioning. Tired of having no answers.

Perhaps now was the time to get those answers, take a little power back for herself.

'What exactly did we talk about that night?' she asked, for the first time not caring how demanding she sounded.

One of his perfectly arched, soot-black brows rose, that glint in his eyes becoming more pronounced. 'Are you sure it's our conversation you want to know about?'

Lark took another silent breath, the ache inside her intensifying. If she was honest with herself, although she did want to know what they'd talked about it, it was the other stuff she kept thinking about.

Other stuff? Such as how exactly you ended up in his bed and what you did there?

A flush crept into her cheeks. She wished she could deny those thoughts too, yet she couldn't. Her brain couldn't stop thinking about them. No, she needed to know. He was here and he could tell her, and she would be a fool to let the opportunity pass.

'I want to know everything,' she said. 'Everything we did.'

'Everything hmmm?' He studied her in that unnerving way a moment more, then leaned forward, his hands clasped between his knees, his gaze on hers. 'Well, first we talked. About books and movies. About the media and world events. About politics and scientific advances.' He paused. 'We also talked about our lives.'

Oh, God. What on earth had she told him about herself? 'What about our lives?'

'You told me about your mother and your years on the run spent hiding from your father in Australia. About what a wonderful mother she'd been to you, yet how fragile, and how you had to take care of her because of her mental health.'

Oh, no. It was worse than she'd thought. She'd literally spilled her guts to him. What had he done to make her trust him that way? She didn't understand. She might have understood if she'd met him *after* the accident, because then she could explain her apparent openness with him as a side effect of the brain injury. But not *before*.

'Why on earth would I have told you any of that?' she asked.

'We'd had a cognac or two and you told me you were in Rome because you'd just lost your mother and had wanted a holiday to get away. So I told you that I too had just lost my aunt.'

That did not make her feel any better.

She'd shared everything of herself with him and he still remembered. Yet while he might have shared with her, she'd forgotten. She'd forgotten everything. Tension gripped her.

'I was drunk?' She didn't want to ask, but she made herself. 'Is that what you're saying?'

'No.' His gaze very direct. 'You weren't drunk. I wouldn't have taken you to bed if you had been, please believe that.'

She had no reason at all to believe that, yet there was no doubting the look in his eyes. He meant what he said.

A small thread of relief wound through her. 'Okay, so if I wasn't drunk, why would I have told you all of that?'

'Because you were lonely and wanted someone to talk to, and we had a common experience.'

Lark shifted uncomfortably in her seat, remembering the family she'd seen at the Colosseum and how lonely that had made her feel. How the realisation had settled down in her that now that her mother was gone, she was essentially alone in the world. She didn't have any siblings and since her mother's parents were dead, the only other family she had was her father. But she had no desire whatsoever to connect with him.

For some reason, though, the person she'd chosen to connect with was sitting across from her now, in the shape of this arrogant, maddening, devastatingly attractive man.

'Why on earth would I chose you?' she asked.

'Let me remind you.' That smoky glint in his eyes glittered and he reached to take her hand where it lay on the armrest, holding it in his and turning it palm up.

He moved so quickly she had no time to protest and then at the feel of his fingers on her skin, she found she couldn't speak anyway. It was as if the humming static of his touch had deprived her of speech.

'I had just told you that I lost the aunt who'd brought me up,' he murmured, holding her hand in his much bigger one, his fingers long and blunt and capable. 'And you leaned forward and took my hand just like this.'

His touch was warm and he cradled her hand gently in his, stopping her breath. And she knew she should pull away, but for some reason she could only sit there as he brushed his thumb over her palm. The contact sent a burst of sensual electricity crackling over her skin and every thought flew straight out of her head.

She swallowed, staring into the vivid blue of his eyes.

'We stared at each other,' he went. 'Just like this. With our hands touching.'

'And then what happened?' she heard herself ask.

'And then?' The hungry glitter in his eyes was the only warning she got. 'Then I did this.'

And before she could move, he pulled her out of her chair and into his lap.

* * *

Cesare was playing with fire and he knew it. Yet he hadn't been able to help himself. He'd been exquisitely aware of her presence since the moment they'd boarded the plane. She'd been sitting bolt upright in her seat, studying the agreement he'd drawn up with fierce attention, and he knew that sitting near her would be a mistake. That he might try something ill-advised, something that he shouldn't do such as reminding her again of their night together.

He shouldn't, not when it was easier all round if those memories stayed forgotten. Yet there was a part of him—and no prizes for guessing which part—that desperately wanted her to remember every single second of the night she'd spent in his bed.

So he'd paced up and down the aisle of the plane, talking to various people, including his closest friend, Aristophanes Katsaros, renowned mathematical genius and self-made billionaire owner of one of the biggest finance companies on the planet.

Aristophanes, who rarely paid much attention to anything that wasn't equations or financial algorithms and had long made it known that he wasn't interested in having a family of his own, had been congratulatory about Cesare's new fatherhood status. But also dismissive of Cesare's self-control when it came to Lark.

'What does it matter if you have her again?' he'd said in his usual bored way. 'It means nothing, not if you don't want it to. Sleep with her or don't, another woman will come along in a couple of days anyway.'

Aristophanes was famous for having his assistants choose and manage his lovers, including putting them into his schedule, since he was far too busy to manage them himself. Cesare had asked him on more than one occasion what he did if his assistants chose someone he wasn't attracted to and Aristophanes had merely shrugged and told him that was impossible, since his assistants rigorously followed the checklist Aristophanes had given them.

Cesare still didn't understand, but then he didn't expect Aristophanes to understand why he was reluctant to have another night with Lark.

He barely understood himself. That night had been special, yet his doubts about repeating it had only made it even more so and he couldn't allow that.

Aristophanes was right about one thing: a repeat performance meant nothing, only that he'd enjoyed the sex and wanted to do it again. So really, did it matter if he wanted to sit down close to her? If he wanted to talk to her about that night? If he wanted to touch her?

More wisps of honey-gold hair had come out of her ponytail and the pink roses on her blouse made her pale skin even pinker, highlighting the blush that stained her cheeks whenever he looked at her. Those sea-green eyes of hers had flashed with annoyance and it satisfied him unreasonably that her annoyance was because of him.

He'd liked that he affected her and he'd liked it even more when she'd started asking him what they'd talked about that night and getting angry. He knew that anger was because she thought she didn't want to know and yet hadn't been able to stop herself from asking.

He'd also been conscious of the way she'd watched him as he'd paced up and down the jet's aisle while talking to Aristophanes. She hadn't wanted to do that either, yet her gaze kept being drawn to him all the same.

She wanted him.

He remembered that light in her eyes, how the flecks of blue in her green eyes had glittered bright and hot when he'd pulled her into his arms. The same way they'd glittered when he'd kissed her a couple of hours back in his palazzo, and when he'd put his hand over hers just before.

The same way they were glittering now.

She was breathing very fast, her body a soft warm weight in his lap, her vanilla scent winding around him, making him relive that night all over again.

'What are you doing?' she asked, eyes wide.

'You wanted to know what happened,' he said. 'I'm telling you.'

'I don't recall asking for a demonstration.'

Her cheeks were deeply flushed, the pulse at the base of her throat beating fast. Her golden ponytail was draped over his shoulder, golden strands catching in the dark blue wool, and he felt a sudden and deep possessiveness grip him, making him tighten his hold.

'You really don't want to remember this?' he asked. 'You came into my lap that night without a protest, just the way you did now. And then you wound your arms around my neck and kissed me as if you hadn't been able to think of anything else except the way I'd taste.'

Her throat moved, her gaze locked with his. She'd softened against him, making all the blood in his veins rush below his belt. The pressure of her lovely rear against his groin making him ache.

He wanted her, he couldn't deny it. That morning

when he'd returned to his villa and found his bed empty, he'd told himself he was glad. He hadn't wanted another night. He'd been there, done that, and trying to track her down was a fool's game.

He didn't chase women, not ever, and he wasn't going to change his habits just for her.

So he'd pushed her out of his thoughts, made himself forget.

But he hadn't forgotten. That night had imprinted itself on his memory and for the past two years, he hadn't been able to stop measuring every other woman he'd slept with against her. And it didn't matter how lovely or passionate or sexually inventive those women had been, something about them always came up short.

He'd told himself it wasn't because they weren't her, of course not. That night had been different because of his complicated feelings around the death of his aunt, leaving him the last Donati, nothing else. They weren't because she was special or different.

Yet looking down into her eyes now, he had to accept that perhaps she *had* been different. That the night they'd spent together *had* been special. And that he did want to revisit it after all.

It wouldn't be the same. She had no memory of their connection and while he did, he couldn't forget that she was the mother of his child.

You really want to complicate that *with sex? Especially when she's clearly angry with you?*

She might be angry with him, but she still wanted him; he could see the desire flickering in her eyes. And after all, what was complicated about sex? For the past couple of months, he hadn't found himself a lover, telling himself that he was too busy. But he knew deep down that he hadn't found himself a lover because he was still searching for the experience he'd had that night, of Lark in his arms and the pleasure he'd found with her.

Now it was all he could think about.

Here she was and what they'd had that night, they could have again. Or if not that, then something similar. Where would be the harm? It could even be a good thing. Once those test results came back and Maya was revealed as his daughter, they would end up having to deal with things like custody and living arrangements, and he already had a couple of ideas about how he'd like to manage that.

In fact, he'd been thinking about it almost exclusively since he'd arranged for this little agreement to be drawn up and for the jet to be prepared.

'I might have done then,' she said. 'But I don't care how you taste right now.'

'No?' He raised a brow. 'Then why are you staring at my mouth?'

She flushed an even deeper pink, her gaze instantly lifting, her chin getting very set. 'I wasn't looking—'

'Would it be the worst thing in the world to admit that you want me?' he interrupted, tired of her denials all of a sudden. 'You had no problem letting me know that night. In fact, you didn't want to leave my bed.'

'Will you stop talking about that night?'

'Why? Does it make you feel things you don't want to feel?'

'I don't—'

Cesare laid a finger over her soft mouth, silencing her.

Her eyes narrowed, but she made no move to get off

him. Instead, she opened her mouth and bit the tip of his finger.

A knife of sensation slid through him, white-hot and intense. Pure animal desire. The softness of her lips and the sharp edge of her teeth against his skin. And before he knew what he was doing, he'd taken his finger away, bent and covered that soft mouth of hers with his own.

She made a low, angry sound, but her hands were on his shoulders, her fingers digging in, holding him to her and her mouth opened, letting him in, the heat and sweet taste of her filling him.

He was hard instantly, desire gripping him by the throat. A desire he hadn't felt since that night two years ago. And he knew in that moment that it didn't matter how many other women he'd tried to bury that memory with, he'd never be able to bury it. That the only real answer was to relive it. Perhaps if he did, he'd be able to let it go once and for all.

Her mouth was so hot and so sweet and she was kissing him back the way she'd kissed him two years ago in Rome, as if she was starving for him. And he couldn't hold back. He didn't want to. He slid his tongue into her mouth, exploring, tasting, devouring her like the sweet treat she was, and this time the sound that escaped her was a sigh, a whimper of need.

Dio, he remembered that sound. When he'd first kissed her and then when he'd slid his hand beneath her shirt, touching her satiny skin. She'd arched into his palm that night, desperate for his touch, just as she was arching against him now, pressing her breasts against his chest, clearly wanting him just as much as he wanted her.

Her arms slid around his neck, her mouth hungry as

she began to kiss him back, hesitant at first and then getting more needy, her tongue touching his, tasting him, exploring him.

His world began to narrow, hunger taking over, and it didn't matter that they were on his private jet that would be landing very soon, or that he wanted to see the daughter he'd never known he'd had—after all, it wouldn't be the first time he'd had a woman on his jet.

It would be so easy. He could push up the little skirt she wore, slip her underwear aside, and then he could take her in his lap. They wouldn't even have to break this mind-blowing kiss.

And then what? She's already furious with you, do you really want to make it worse? Especially when it's likely you'll have to talk to her about custody once your paternity has been confirmed. Also, have you ever thought that she might be frightened? Having no memory of a sexual experience that made her pregnant mustn't be easy.

Dio, that was all true. Anger, he liked, but he didn't want her afraid.

He broke the kiss and pulled back, staring down at her.

Her head was on his shoulder, her cheeks deeply flushed, her mouth full and red. Her eyes were as dark as a winter sea.

'Do not be afraid of me, Lark,' he said roughly. 'I know you don't trust me, but please trust this if nothing else. I did not hurt you that night and I will not hurt you now. You are safe with me.'

There it was again, the flicker of her temper. 'I'm not afraid of you.'

'Good.' He took a breath that wasn't quite as steady as it should have been. 'Because I want you. Right here. Right now.'

CHAPTER FIVE

THE PIERCING BLUE of Cesare's gaze had gone dark with desire.

For her.

Lark's heart was thundering in her ears, her skin tight, an aching pressure between her thighs. Her mouth felt full and swollen, the stunning effect of his kiss ringing through her.

One minute she'd been sitting there, fighting her anger. The next she was in his lap, surrounded by all that hard muscle and the astonishing heat of his body, his hungry gaze on hers.

She'd thought of making some protest or pushing at him the way she'd done in his palazzo, but something about the way he'd looked at her, his heat and the scent of his aftershave had made all her muscles feel heavy and slow. Then his grip had tightened, as if he hadn't wanted to let her go, and the really terrible thing, the terrible truth that had settled down in her, was that she hadn't wanted him to.

She hadn't wanted to admit to the sense of familiarity and recognition as he'd touched her either. The part of her that remembered what it had felt like to be in his arms, to be held by him, to have him close, his mouth on hers. That had felt safe with him, that knew he wouldn't hurt her, and wasn't afraid.

The part of her that *wanted* to remember. That wanted more. That was angry that her first sexual experience had been taken from her by the car that had knocked her down.

And it must have been good experience too, judging from the way he kissed you.

It wasn't fair that had been taken from her, it just wasn't, and as she'd thought just before, she was tired of not knowing. Tired of fighting herself too, because shouldn't she know? She'd talked to him, fine, but what about afterwards? When he'd kissed her and she'd kissed him back, and then he'd taken her to bed?

What had it been like? She'd experienced his kiss and to feel his mouth on hers had been so…good. But what about his touch? His hands on her bare skin? She wanted more and it was time to admit that.

He knew all these things about her and she knew nothing, and that was wrong. Yes, that gave him power and she was tired of him having all of it. Because it wasn't only the memory of that night he had, but a family legacy that went back centuries, massive wealth, and looks good enough to tempt an angel into sin. He also had authority and arrogance, and all she had was…what?

She had her child and a decent job, it was true. The flat she lived in was okay, but it was slightly run-down and there was no garden. Certainly it couldn't compare to his palazzo.

It's not just getting answers to your questions that will give you power. He wants you and that gives you power too.

The thought wound through her like champagne fizzing in her blood.

Looking up at him, she could see the need in his eyes. The hunger. Yes, he wanted her. Right now, right here, he'd said.

They'd had one night two years ago and this powerful man, this man who had everything, hadn't been able to forget her.

There *was* power in that. Power over him.

Power and knowledge and *him.*

She might not ever get the memories of that night back, but that didn't mean she couldn't create new ones. She could give herself that couldn't she? Especially if he could make her feel as good as she suspected he could. As good as she had the night she didn't remember.

The admission eased something tight inside her, as if she'd been holding herself contained since the moment she'd met him, and now she didn't have to.

Now she could take what she wanted too.

But she wouldn't let him have it all his own way. She'd exert some of that newfound power of hers, see how that would affect him. Chip away at his arrogance. Make him wait. Make him sweat. Make him desperate.

Why not? There was also a power in not remembering too, because while she might not know the details, her body remembered. And she didn't feel nervous or unsure, because she'd already done this once. She knew he wanted her, that he hadn't been able to forget the one night he'd had with her. Which meant it had been good. Very good.

He'd buried the fingers of one hand in her hair, closing them into a fist, holding her tight, and she could feel his desperation in the strength of his grip. For the first time since they'd met, a sense of satisfaction filled her.

'Now?' she asked huskily. 'This is hardly private.'

'I'll tell my staff to stay up the front of the plane. They won't bother us.'

She lifted a hand and touched his cheekbone experimentally, her heart racing, feeling the warm satin of his skin and the faint prickle of whiskers. It felt thrilling, almost illicit to touch him like this.

Nipping his finger when he'd touched her mouth had been an automatic reaction, and she hadn't known where the urge had come from. Perhaps that was another thing to come out of that night. Whatever, now that she'd had a taste of his skin, all salty and masculine, she wanted more.

She'd never been kissed—or at least not that she remembered—and after hearing her mother talk about how terrible men were, she'd decided she never wanted to go there herself. But now, here she was in the arms of a man who wanted her, and she didn't feel threatened.

No, she felt powerful.

She let her fingers trail down his cheekbone and along his strong jaw, loving the prickle of stubble against her fingertips. Loving, too, the way his gaze flared as she touched him, blue darkening into twilight shadows.

She touched his mouth, tracing the line of his lower lip, the curve of it. It felt soft even though nothing else about him was, and it had felt soft too when he'd kissed her. Yet also firm, masterful…

He'd gone very still, making no move as she touched him, her fingers trailing where they would, his gaze fixed to hers. She traced the proud line of his nose then up to those sooty black brows with their arrogant arch, and back down again to his other cheekbone.

'Little bird.' His hold in her hair tightened. 'I'm getting impatient. Yes or no. Give me an answer.'

She liked that he asked her. She liked that despite him pulling her into his lap and kissing her, he'd waited for her to respond before he did anything more. Her mother had always told her that men took what they wanted, took what they thought was theirs, yet despite his obvious power and wealth, he was waiting for her to give him permission.

Maybe this was a glimpse of the man she'd met that night two years ago. The man whom she'd wanted enough to give him her virginity in spite of all the warnings about men her mother had given her.

'I'm thinking,' she said, flexing that power a little, wanting to see how far she could push him. 'I'm also trying to remember.' She stroked her fingers down the side of his strong neck to the knot of his tie, then pulled at it, the silk loosening, baring his throat. His pulse beat there, strong and steady beneath her fingertips, his skin warm.

She heard his breath catch at her touch, saw his eyes darken even further.

'Shall I tell you what happened after you kissed me?' he asked softly. 'After you wound your arms around my neck?'

Her own breathing was getting faster, the ache between her thighs a growing pressure.

'Yes,' she said, her mouth dry.

Blue flames leapt in his eyes. 'I did this.' He dropped one hand to the buttons of her blouse. 'I opened the shirt you were wearing.' He flicked the top button open. 'One button at a time.' Another one. 'I went slowly, because I didn't want to scare you.' A third button. 'And also, because I wanted to tantalise you.' A fourth.

Her heart beat like thunder in her head, her skin sensitised. She couldn't stop looking at his face, at the hunger etched in stark lines there, and all for her.

Cool air whispered over her skin as the fabric parted, making her shiver.

'And then,' he went on, undoing the last button so her blouse was entirely open. 'I spread out the fabric so I could see you.' He pushed the two halves of her blouse wide, baring the white lace of her bra. 'Your nipples were hard. Just like they are now, and I touched them. Like this.' His fingertips grazed over the peaks of her breasts, first one and then the other, and sensation crackled through her, a knife of pleasure that tore a gasp from her throat.

She felt half hypnotised by his touch and by the deep roughened sound of his voice. By the pressure between her thighs that made her want to shift restlessly beneath his touch.

'After that,' he murmured, 'since your bra had a front clasp just like this one, I did this…' With a twist of his fingers, he flicked open her bra and the material fell away, the air cool on her sensitised nipples.

Lark took a sharp breath as he gazed down at her, desire glittering in his eyes. 'You were so beautiful that night,' he continued. 'As beautiful as you are now, and so I touched you just like this…' He cupped one breast in his hot palm, squeezing her gently, teasing her nipple with his thumb and drawing a shudder from her. 'Then I had to taste you, because you looked so delicious.'

He bent, his tongue touching her aching nipple and making her gasp aloud. Then he drew it into his mouth, applying gentle pressure, and she groaned.

This wasn't going as she'd planned. She'd wanted to push him further, flex her power even more, but she'd become a victim of her own hunger and now she didn't want him to stop. Not when it felt so good. Familiar, too, though her memory of that night was still a black hole. Her body knew, though. Her body was greeting him as if it had been starved for his touch, aching for him. Desperate for him.

Her eyes fluttered closed, her world narrowing to the heat of his mouth on her breast, his fingers in her hair holding her exactly where he wanted her, his hard thighs beneath her, surrounded by his powerful body.

God, she loved it.

Weren't you supposed to the one making him *desperate?*

Oh, but did that really matter now? She didn't care about power games, not in this moment. In this moment all she wanted was him.

She groaned and arched her back, pressing herself into his mouth. Her fingers slid into his hair, the strands feeling like raw silk, soft yet with a delicious roughness to it.

'Do you remember, little bird?' he whispered against her heated skin. 'Do you remember me doing this to you?'

'No,' she replied, breathless. 'But keep going. What else did we do?'

He raised his head, the shadows in his eyes darkening into midnight. 'You have to say yes, Lark. I'm not going to show you anything more until you do.'

You were supposed to make him beg...

The thought drifted through her pleasure-fogged brain, but she couldn't remember why she'd wanted that. And anyway, all she had to say was yes and she couldn't think of a single reason to refuse him.

'Yes,' she whispered.

'Yes, what?'

'Yes, Signor Donati. Right here. Right now.'

His beautiful mouth curved, amusement warring with the satisfaction glinting in his eyes. 'I like Signor Donati, believe me. But that night you called me Cesare.'

'Cesare,' she echoed, his name sounding like music. 'Yes, Cesare.'

The amusement vanished, heat flaring hot and bright in his eyes. 'One moment,' he said, then shifted, getting his phone from his pocket. He hit a couple of buttons then issued an order in clipped Italian before throwing the phone down in the seat next to them.

'I've instructed my staff to not to bother us,' he said. 'We have privacy.' His gaze took on an intent look. 'Now, little bird. Why don't you take the rest of your clothes off for me?'

Lark shivered all over, her mouth going dry. 'Is that what I did that night?' she asked in a hoarse voice. 'After you t-touched me?'

Slowly he shook his head. 'I undressed you that night. But I wished I'd had the patience to watch you undress for me.'

She wanted to. She wanted to see more of that hunger etched on his face, more of his desire for her as she took her clothes off, baring herself for him. She'd missed out that night and she didn't want to miss out again.

So she slid off his lap and stood in front of his seat, reaching for the zip on her skirt and pulling it down. She felt no hesitation, no embarrassment. He'd seen her naked before and he'd liked it—he'd already told her so and anyway, there was nothing but heat in his eyes now. It didn't take a genius to work out that he was already loving what he saw.

She slid her skirt down, taking her knickers with it, then stepped out of the fabric, kicking off her little heels. She eased her blouse off and her bra, until finally she stood naked before him.

He sat back in his seat and let out a long breath, staring at her as if he wanted to eat her alive. 'Come here,' he ordered, soft and rough.

But now she could feel it, that power. He might have called the shots just before, but this—all of it—lived and died by her will and only hers.

Lark gave him a slow smile then stepped forward, easing herself into his lap, sitting astride him so she faced him. Making sure she took it slow and easy, watching as the fire in his eyes leapt, his hunger burning bright as she settled herself on him.

'Ah, *Dio…*' he breathed, his gaze dropping down her naked body then returning to her face. 'I remember this. So beautiful…' He lifted his hands, cupping her breasts and she sighed, arching into his palms, wanting more of his touch. 'Say my name,' he said, demanding. 'Tell me how much you want me.'

'Cesare…' She caressed every syllable, loving how it made the fire in his eyes burn bright. 'I want you…' There was power in this too, in admitting her hunger for him, because that fuelled his, she could see it in his beautiful face.

It made her want to goad him even more. She reached down between them, her hand sliding over the fly of his suit trousers, finding him hot and hard beneath her, and lord…he was impressive.

He groaned as she squeezed him experimentally and she loved the sound, loved that she could draw it out of him.

'Lark,' he said roughly. 'If you continue doing that, I won't be responsible for what happens next.'

'What does happen next?' The words were breathless as she squeezed him again. 'I can't quite remember.'

'Witch,' he growled and lifted both hands, burying his fingers in her hair and pulling her in for a kiss, devouring her like a man starved.

He tasted like heaven. Like brandy or some other wickedly alcoholic sweet drink and it went straight to her head. Her arms lifted and she was twining them around his neck and arching against him, pressing her exquisitely sensitive nipples against the wool of his jacket.

There was something unbearably erotic in being naked while he was still fully dressed. It didn't make her feel weak. It made her feel as if she was the powerful one, using her sexuality and his own desire against him, bringing him to his knees.

'Say my name,' she whispered against his mouth, consciously imitating him. 'Tell me how much you want me.'

'Lark,' he murmured, the word rough and bitten off. 'And how about I show you instead.' Then he pulled her hands away from his fly and freed himself from his trousers. From somewhere he produced a condom packet that he ripped open with practiced ease. Then he sheathed himself before sliding one hand between her thighs, stroking her hot wet flesh, making her cry out as a flood of pleasure nearly overwhelmed her.

Then without another word, he positioned himself and thrust inside her.

She gasped, her head falling back, pleasure flooding her at the delicious stretch and burn of him inside her. She heard the sound of his harshly indrawn breath and he went still. His hand in her hair tightened and he pulled her mouth to his, kissing her with a hunger and passion that drove the last shreds of thought from her head.

She kissed him back desperately as he began to move, deep and slow, a rhythm that had her shifting on him, trying to match it. He dropped a hand to her bare hip, his palm burning against her skin, showing her the way, and then she found it. A rise and fall that was gentle at first and slow, then gaining pace.

Lark moaned against his mouth, as the pleasure became more and more intense, his hand on her hip pressing hard, his fingertips digging into her bare flesh even as his fist in her hair tightened still further, holding her still.

She put her palms flat to his chest, her nails against his skin, kissing him back hungrily as the pleasure rose in an agonising wave inside her. They moved faster, his thrusts harder, and then he slipped a hand between her thighs, stroking the sensitive bundle of nerves there and she came apart, crying his name as the climax took her and swept her away.

It was the sound of his name, hoarse and full of breathless pleasure, that catapulted him over the edge. As Lark sagged against him, he drove himself harder and faster inside her, both hands now on her hips to keep her still and then, long before he was ready for it, the orgasm hit him with all the force of a freight train, and he pulled her mouth to his as it took him, muffling the sound of his own release with her lips.

Afterwards he couldn't move. He could hardly breathe. She was a warm weight on him, her small, curvy body leaning against his chest, her face pressed to his shoulder. His fingers were wound in her hair, the strands soft and silky against his skin and he could smell her vanilla scent tinged with sweet feminine musk and sex.

Dio. He hadn't expected that to happen so fast. But tasting her mouth and then her pretty breasts, and then watching her as she'd taken off her clothes for him before sitting naked in his lap, her sea-green eyes dark with desire…

It had been a long time without sex for him and every other woman he'd been with since that night had been somehow…unsatisfying. Not that the problem lay with them. He was the issue and he knew it. Or rather, the issue was *her.*

Her and what had happened between them that night. The lovers he'd had previously had all been skilled and he'd had pleasure from them. But sex had always been a selfish thing. He could give a woman pleasure, but nothing more, and that was the beginning and end of it.

Not with Lark, though. Lark had been unpractised, a virgin, and so what an experienced woman would understand without a word being said, she wouldn't know. And she wouldn't understand. He'd had to be clear with her what he could give her and what he couldn't, and so he'd expected her to give nothing of herself to him, the way his other lovers had.

Yet she hadn't. That night in his arms she'd given him everything. She'd been so generous, giving him her complete and utter trust. He'd never had that before from anyone. He'd never felt as if he held someone's soul in his hands and never wanted to.

He was as his parents had made him, as selfish and self-serving as they were. Unlike them though, he owned it. He didn't pretend. They'd used him in their private war against each other, telling him that they cared about him, that they were doing this for him, but they weren't. He was the weapon they aimed at each other and when that weapon no longer had the power to hurt, they'd discarded him.

Everything he did, his every action was on them. He'd been going to tear apart their precious Donati legacy and plough any leftover ashes into the ground, take his revenge for how his father had locked him away for months in order to punish his mother. How his mother had then tried to kill him in order to hurt his father. She'd failed at that luckily, but not before his father had shot her and then himself.

Really, the whole thing had been almost farcical in its drama, so was it any wonder he'd turned out the way he had?

Of course, now he had an heir, things were different and he'd changed his mind about his revenge, but that still didn't mean he could be trusted with anyone's soul. He didn't want to be trusted anyway, and he was glad that this time Lark hadn't been so emotionally honest. She'd been angry and guarded with him since the moment she'd got on the plane, and he suspected the passion she'd let out to play hadn't been so much about him as about herself.

He wasn't complaining, though. He was familiar with the heat that lay beneath the surface of her cheerful smiles, and when she'd slid her hand down over the front of his trousers, desire darkening the green of her eyes, he'd felt nothing but pure satisfaction that she was giving in to it. She hadn't hesitated in touching him, her boldness gripping him by the throat and not letting go.

She'd pushed him, demanding he repeat the same words he'd ordered from her, and he had, without protest. Perhaps he shouldn't have allowed her that power, yet her response had been so very gratifying….

She shifted in his lap, but he tightened his arms around her, keeping her where she was.

He wanted to hold her a bit longer, his brain already running through plans about how he could have this again, keep her naked like this and in his arms. Not for ever, naturally, but for enough time that he didn't feel this nagging need. That he could finally look at other women and feel desire for them the way he used to instead of being consumed by thoughts of Lark.

And why couldn't he have this again? What was stopping them from sleeping with each other when the need arose? They had significant chemistry and gave each other great pleasure. She could hardly say no to that.

Her fingers spread on his chest, pressing herself away and this time he reluctantly released his hold. She lifted her head, her cheeks pink, her hair coming out of its ponytail, all mussed by the grip of his hands. She looked thoroughly and totally ravished, the mere sight of her making him hard.

'I think,' she began in a husky voice. 'That that was a mist—'

'No,' he interrupted abruptly. 'No, it was *not* a mistake.' He lifted his hands and cupped her face, her skin like silk against his palms. 'It was perfect, little bird. Just as the night we spent together was perfect.'

She flushed. 'It can't happen again.'

'Why not?'

A breath escaped her and she pulled away, sliding out of his lap and reaching for her discarded clothing. 'Because I don't want it to.' She turned and began to dress. 'What I wanted was to remember that night or at least what it felt like to have sex with you. I still don't remember, but at least now I've had sex with you. I don't need another demonstration and especially not when we still have the issue of this stupid paternity test to deal with.'

She kept her face turned resolutely away, a thread of emotion in her voice that made him want to reach for her, turn her so he could look into her eyes and see what it was.

But that wasn't keeping it just about sex. That was engaging and he didn't want to engage, especially not with anything resembling emotion.

If she didn't want to sleep with him again, that was fine. It didn't matter and why would it? When he could get pleasure from anyone? He only had to crook a finger and women came running, so this one's refusal shouldn't affect him at all.

Yet he couldn't deny that something like frustration coiled like a snake inside him. Frustration at being denied. Frustration because he wanted more, wanted her and only her. No one else would do.

If she hadn't been so passionate with him then he'd have accepted that no and never thought of her again. But she *had* been passionate with him. She'd come apart so beautifully in his arms, crying his name, and she was fooling herself if she thought she didn't want him again. Still Maya was a legitimate reason for her not to want anything more from him, and even though it was to his detriment, he admired her for putting her daughter ahead of her own desires. Unlike his mother, who'd fed him poison purely to punish his father.

Perhaps Lark would think differently once she'd accepted that he was Maya's father. Whatever the case, he certainly wasn't going to chase her. No, he wanted her to come to him. Still, that didn't mean he couldn't weigh the dice in his favour.

'Once on a plane is not really enough to know what sex with me is like,' he said, watching her dress, unable to take his gaze off her. It felt like a loss when she covered up all that pretty bare skin.

She gave him a sidelong look as she put on her bra then began to do up the buttons of her blouse. 'Did I mention how arrogant you are?'

He ignored that, leisurely dealing with the condom and his own clothes, not missing how she kept glancing at the movement of his hands as if she too couldn't keep her eyes off him. 'I'd reserve judgement until we have a bed if I were you.'

'But you're not me and my judgement is just fine, thank you very much.'

Cesare studied her, noting her pink her cheeks and

the slight tremble of her hands. Remembering the way she'd clutched at him and how she'd cried his name as she came.

She'd wanted him very much and he suspected she still did, but she didn't want to admit it.

'Why is it so hard to admit you still want me, little bird?' he asked idly. 'I still want you.'

Her flush deepened. 'Because I don't. I was curious to see what sex with you was like and now I know. Curiosity satisfied.'

'Really? We had a whole night before. This was a mere fifteen minutes. Barely enough time to even get started.'

'It was enough for me.' She smoothed down her skirt and then sat opposite him, lifting her hands to deal with her hair, her lashes veiling her gaze.

And Cesare's frustration pulled tight inside him. She was lying or at the very least hiding something and no matter what he'd told himself about not engaging, he wasn't having it. Pushing himself out of his seat, he took a step over to where she sat and put his hands on the arms of her seat. Then he leaned down, getting into her space, his face inches from hers.

Her eyes went wide before darkening, her gaze dipping helplessly to his mouth.

'Really?' he murmured, satisfaction clenching inside him. 'Tell me you aren't thinking about kissing me again, having me inside you again, and maybe this time when we're both naked.'

Fire leapt in her eyes, the pulse at the base of her throat beating hard and fast. 'I'm not.'

'Yes, you were. Do you really want me to prove it to you?'

She took a little breath. ‘I…no.’

‘Then tell me, Lark. Tell me you still want me. You had no problem with saying the words when I had you in my arms. Why is it so difficult now?’

‘Because…’ Her chest rose and fell as if she was fighting something. ‘Being with you made me realise what I’d missed out on. My first sexual experience and I don’t remember it. I don’t remember you. And what we just had now was…amazing, but it was also angry and fraught, and I don’t like being angry. I don’t like how you manage to get under my skin.’

Her honesty hit him in a place he wasn’t expecting. A place that remembered that night and how special it had been. There had been no tension between them except delicious sexual tension and neither of them had been guarded or angry with the other. There had been pleasure and an intimacy he hadn’t known he’d wanted until it had happened.

An intimacy he could not and would not have again.

He regretted that she didn’t remember, he realised all of a sudden. He regretted that she had no memories of their intimacy or closeness, or of the passion they’d shared. It was a loss for both of them.

‘I’m sorry, little bird,’ he said after a moment, and he meant it. ‘I’m sorry you don’t remember that night. But I don’t mind your anger. In fact, be angry with me all you want. Scream at me, shout at me, show me your claws. I like it.’

She stared up at him, searching his face for what he didn’t know. ‘I know what you’re trying to do,’ she said, her voice husky. ‘And it won’t work. I’m still not going to sleep with you again.’

Except she wanted to, he knew. He could see the truth in her eyes.

Why she was insisting on refusing him, he didn't know, but clearly it had something to do with her feelings around her lost memories.

He couldn't argue with that.

You don't need to sleep with her again. Sex is not *just sex for her and that makes it complicated. Disengage, remember?*

'Well,' he murmured. 'Far be it from me to insist.' His hands tightened on the arms of her seat momentarily, then pushed himself away from her and straightened to his full height. 'If you change your mind, you only have to ask.'

Yet more colour crept through her cheeks. 'Don't worry, I won't be changing my mind.'

For a moment, he stayed where he was, staring down at her, seeing the passion that lay deep inside her, burning like banked embers in her eyes. All it would take would be another touch, another kiss, and she'd go up in flames…

But no. He wasn't going to touch her again.

He smiled. 'Fine. If you do, though, let me know. I think you'd look pretty on your knees.'

Then he turned around, took his phone from his pocket and began to make the last of his phone calls.

CHAPTER SIX

LARK'S PALMS WERE sweaty as she sat her at tiny kitchen table, unable to concentrate on the crossword puzzle she was trying to do to pass the time.

Cesare—no, *Signor Donati*—would be here any minute and all the things she'd told herself she was going to do that morning hadn't got done, because she hadn't been able to settle.

Maya was playing in her playpen in the little living area just across the hall and Lark could hear the happy sounds she was making as she smashed a couple of wooden blocks together. She hadn't started walking yet, but she wasn't far off and Lark knew her playpen days were numbered. Which meant Lark's life was going to get a little bit more difficult.

There was a thump then a cry, and instantly Lark leapt to her feet, her crossword forgotten. She went into the living room to find Maya sitting on her bottom and crying loudly, lifting her arms to Lark as she appeared.

Lark went over and picked her daughter up, murmuring comfortingly as she cuddled her close. Maya was getting heavy now and of course as soon as she was picked up, she wanted to go back down. She was a very strong-willed little girl and stubborn to boot.

Like her father, perhaps?

Lark kissed the top of Maya's rose-gold head, trying to ignore the anger that lay like a stone in the pit of her stomach. She didn't want to think about Cesare Donati and she especially didn't want to think of him as Maya's father.

The night before, after the plane had landed, she'd been terribly afraid he'd insist on coming back to her flat with her and seeing Maya. Either that or convincing her to come back to whatever palatial London house he occupied for the night.

She'd been too honest with him on the plane, when he'd loomed over her, surrounding her with his heat and his scent. Her mouth had gone dry and all she'd been able to think about was kissing him again, having him again. She'd wanted to tell him that the sex had meant nothing, her curiosity had been satisfied, but he'd surprised the truth out of her.

Deep down she'd been hoping against hope that sex with him would return her memories, yet it hadn't. That night was still a black hole. And now she'd had a taste of what she'd missed out on that night with him. What it must have been like that first time, to kiss him, touch him. Have him inside her. Those moments in the plane had been like missing pieces of the jigsaw puzzle falling into place, and yet... The whole picture remained hidden.

Being with him again would only remind her of all those other moments she'd lost, that she'd never get back. Of seeing his first reaction to her body, then the joy of mutual discovery, the thrill of newness, of shared wonder...

That was all gone and it had hurt more than she'd expected it to.

She hadn't wanted to tell him any of that, but she had, and there had been recognition in his eyes. And genuine understanding. And pity.

'I'm sorry,' he'd said…

That had made her ache, which in turn had made her angry all over again. She hadn't wanted him to be sorry, she'd wanted him to leave her alone, take his intense, distracting presence elsewhere. She had to look forward, not backwards, and sleeping with him again would definitely be going backwards.

Anyway, as it turned out, he'd neither insisted on coming home with her nor tried to tempt her into coming home with him.

As soon as they'd disembarked the plane, he'd told her he'd see her the next day and a car would take her home. Then he'd walked off, his phone stuck to his ear, got in another car and had been driven away.

She'd told herself she was glad, that she didn't want him anywhere near her. Yet that night, after she'd got home and the nanny had left, and she'd checked on her little girl, she'd gone to sleep and her dreams had been full of him. His hands and his mouth on her. His bare skin against hers. Stroking her, teasing her, taunting her. And then he'd whisper, 'Beg me, little bird,' before vanishing.

She'd woken up aching and restless and in a terrible temper.

Getting tied up in knots over a man, no matter how attractive, was a mistake and one she had to avoid at all costs. She wouldn't be her mother, falling in love with an awful man, marrying him and having his baby only to find herself trapped. Knowing that the only way to protect her child was to run and then be hunted to the ends of the earth.

Okay, so maybe Cesare—*Signor Donati*—wasn't quite as awful as her father had been. But he was terrible all the same. He was forceful, opinionated, arrogant and selfish, and those were enough red flags for her.

What if he's Maya's father?

Then she'd cross that bridge when she came to it. She just didn't want to think about it now.

As if on cue, the doorbell rang. Lark settled Maya on her hip and went to the door to open it, trying to ignore the nerves that leapt and jumped around inside her.

Sure enough, it was him. Cesare Donati. Standing on the doorstep wearing an immaculate handmade suit of dark grey wool. His shirt was black this time, his tie the same deep blue as Maya's eyes.

Behind him, a limo waited at the kerb, looking extremely out of place in her small suburban street, a couple of bodyguards standing nearby.

Not that she was really taking in the limo, not when he was bare inches away.

She'd thought that maybe she'd dreamed his effect on her, that after a night away from him, the force of his presence wouldn't be so intense, but she was wrong.

The impact of him was almost physical.

Her heartbeat sped up, nervousness coiling and tangling inside her. Then his blue gaze locked with hers and a flood of heat washed through her.

All she could remember were those moments on the plane, sitting naked in his lap. His mouth on hers, his fingers clenched tight in her hair. Of him inside her, moving deep and slow, and the intense pleasure uncurling inside her…

'*Buongiorno*, little bird,' he said in his deep, rich voice, his eyes glittering as if he was remembering the same thing. Then his attention shifted, the pressure of it releasing almost making her gasp aloud, and he stared at Maya instead.

He went very still, utterly transfixed by the sight of her, and Lark was overcome with an urge to shield her daughter from the intensity of his gaze. And she might have if Maya hadn't been gazing back, studying him with the same intentness.

There was a moment's silence.

'May I hold her?' Cesare asked unexpectedly, his voice hoarse, still not taking his eyes off Maya.

Lark's first instinct was to refuse. Then again, he'd asked her politely enough and she knew he wouldn't hurt Maya. He'd promised he wouldn't take her away either, and while she didn't trust him, she was starting to think he might actually be a man of his word. He'd had that agreement drawn up, after all, and given his power, he didn't have to do that.

She glanced down at Maya. She wasn't a clingy child, though she had a certain reserve, and usually it took a little while for her to warm to someone. 'If she wants to go,' Lark said.

But it seemed that Maya didn't mind, going to him without a protest, seemingly as fascinated by Cesare as he was by her. In fact, she stared up at him as if she'd never seen anything so incredible in her life.

Then Lark saw the look on Cesare's face as he stared down at the child in his arms. Undisguised awe. Wonder. Amazement. He murmured something in Italian, not making a single protest as the little girl clutched at his suit with a hand covered in mashed banana.

And Lark's heart ached in response. Because she knew how he felt. She'd felt all those emotions too, the moment she'd first cradled her daughter in her arms.

Cesare settled Maya on his hip as if he'd been carrying babies all his life and glanced at Lark. 'Shall we go?'

Lark's stomach clenched. 'Go? Go where?'

'I thought it would better if we conducted this at my residence here in London. I want to spend a little more time with her and there is more privacy from the press there.'

A thread of panic wound through her and she took a half step towards him. 'No, what? Wait, I didn't agree to you taking her anywhere.'

He frowned, his blue gaze searching hers. 'I told you I would never take her from you and I meant it,' he said quietly. 'You will be coming with me. We'll go to my residence where some of Maya's genetic material will be taken and there we'll wait for the results. If the result is negative then you'll take her home. If the result is positive, we'll talk.'

He sounded so reasonable and yet the panic inside her refused to ease. All she could think about was how difficult would it be to run with her daughter, to go somewhere he couldn't find them, to hide Maya from him.

Do you really want your daughter to have the same upbringing you did?

Lark swallowed. Her childhood hadn't been the best, but Grace had done what she could. Yet Lark didn't want Maya growing up with the same fear. Growing up without friends or a safe space. Of never being able to put down roots because you never knew when you'd have to move on.

Maya reached up to Cesare's tie with one grubby hand and pulled on it. He paid absolutely zero notice, letting her ruin the silk as if it didn't matter. 'Come with me, Lark,' he said. 'Please. It'll be all right, I promise.'

Please...

He meant it, she heard the promise in his voice. And there it was again, the understanding in his eyes. The understanding she'd seen on the plane when she'd told him why she couldn't sleep with him again and how he affected her.

He knew her history, because she'd told him, and he knew why she was afraid. And for some reason he was trying to ease her fears.

'Okay,' she said, her jangling nerves settling, soothed by the quiet honesty in his voice, and then before she knew what was happening, she found herself walking down the path after him, to the limo that waited in the street.

His driver had already opened the door and Lark could see a child's car seat already in place. The driver said something to Cesare but Cesare shook his head, placing Maya in the car seat himself. Then he glanced back at Lark. 'Will you check she's secure, please? I think it was installed correctly, but I'd like to have you look at it just in case.'

She wasn't sure how he did that. He said he was a selfish man and yet here he was, finding those little threads of panic inside her and easing them with a please and some genuine reassurance, and by asking her opinion on the safety of her child, something that mattered a great deal to her.

A selfish man wouldn't have cared about her feelings. A selfish man wouldn't have even known she was afraid.

'You mean you don't automatically know everything?' she muttered as she leaned in, checking that Maya was belted in properly.

Cesare was standing beside her, his delicious cedar scent and the heat of his body winding around her, clouding her senses. Making her pulse race and her heart beat loud in her ears.

'...if you change your mind, you only have to ask...'

His words from the plane the night before drifted through her head, taunting her, her body's response to him making a mockery of her insistence that she wasn't going to sleep with him again.

But she couldn't give in to her desire, not when there were so many good reasons why she shouldn't, Maya and her future being the most important ones.

Annoyingly, Maya's seat was all good and he'd buckled her in correctly too. Though, being annoyed by that was stupid. She should be pleased, especially where her daughter's safety was concerned.

With an effort, she shoved her anger away and straightened, glancing at him. 'She's secure,' she forced out. 'Thank you for remembering the seat.'

He lifted one powerful shoulder. 'I consulted the nanny from the night before about what Maya might need. She's going to come here to collect some of Maya's important things if you'll allow it. That way we can get to my residence and take the test as soon as possible.'

It seemed ridiculous to be pleased that he'd asked her

if she minded the nanny coming to get Maya's things, when he'd swept in and organised it all already. Nevertheless, she was pleased.

'That's fine,' she said. 'But do you ever get tired of upending people's lives to suit yourself?'

There was unexpected humour in his eyes and it suited him. It suited him far too well. 'Honestly? No.'

She snorted. 'Thought so.'

A soft, deep laugh escaped him, the sound moving over her like a caress. 'Did you really expect me to give you a different answer, little bird?'

But she didn't want to stand there watching the blue glints of amusement dance in his eyes or listen to that unbelievably sexy laugh again, so she only gave him a disdainful look and got into the limo without a word.

Sometime later, the limo pulled up outside a stately house in Kensington. Clearly old and eye-wateringly expensive, it was white, with a black wrought iron paling fence in front and ivy covering the walls.

As Cesare showed her and Maya inside, she caught a glimpse down the wide hallway of a lovely garden out the back, with trees and green lawns. But there was no time to look properly because then he settled her and Maya in one of the huge front rooms. New baby toys were scattered on the pale carpet and Maya squealed delightedly at the sight of them.

Cesare seemed to have vanished, so Lark wiped her daughter's banana-covered hands clean, then set her down, watching as she toddled happily over to a large plastic truck—she loved trucks—and banged it enthusiastically on the floor. She was still banging it when a woman in a white lab coat came in and asked Lark if she could take a swab from Maya's mouth.

Lark nodded and it was over painlessly, Maya going back to her truck as the woman left.

Lark watched her, trying to ignore the slow creep of dread.

You already know he's her father and continuing to deny it is only going to make things worse.

It was true. In which case she needed a plan, because she was sure Cesare already had one.

Upstairs, Cesare paced around in his study, gripped by a strange restlessness he couldn't quite describe. He didn't want to be here. He wanted to be with Maya, watching her play with the toys he'd bought her. Watching her play full stop.

She was amazing. Perfect in every way.

His daughter.

You don't know that for certain.

Oh, he was certain. He'd been certain since the moment he'd seen her photo on Lark's phone, and meeting her in person had only solidified that certainty.

She was a Donati from her curling rose-gold hair to the tips of her tiny toes.

He'd never held a child before and never wanted to, yet as soon as he'd seen her in Lark's arms, he knew his life wouldn't be complete unless she was in his too. And when Lark had given her to him and he'd held her, so small and fragile, he'd looked down into her blue eyes and known in an instant that he'd give his life for hers. Without hesitation. In a heartbeat.

Then he'd had the strangest thought. Had his parents

ever felt that way about him? Had they ever experienced this moment of instant connection? He didn't want to call it love because love was a terrible, toxic thing and there was nothing toxic about Maya.

Perhaps it was protectiveness then, this feeling. A fierce, burning need to keep her from harm even to his own detriment.

No. Your parents never felt that way about you.

They couldn't have, could they? Otherwise they wouldn't have done what they had to him. His mother wouldn't have accused him of loving his father more than her, and his father wouldn't have punished him for being good for his mother.

He didn't care. They were gone now and good riddance to them.

What was important was her. She was the clean slate, the little innocent. Untouched by his family's toxicity, nothing but pure joy. She'd ruined his suit and his tie by grabbing at them with her little banana-covered hands, but he didn't care about that either. He'd wanted to keep holding her, his suit be damned.

Cesare paced around a bit more then reached into his pocket, pulled out his phone and called Aristophanes. His friend answered immediately, as he always did whenever Cesare called him since neither of them liked waiting for the other.

'I gather from this call that you're waiting for the paternity test results?' Aristophanes asked. His Italian was perfect, though there was the faintest hint of his native Athens in his voice.

'Yes,' Cesare said.

'Is that nervousness I hear?'

'Absolutely not.' Cesare reached the door of his study, turned and paced back to his desk. 'I know the outcome already.'

'I see,' Aristophanes said. 'So what is this call in aid of?'

Cesare let out a breath. 'I want to bring her back to Italy. She's a Donati and she needs to be with me. However…' He paused. 'Her mother will have something to say about it.'

And Lark *would* have something to say about it. And it probably wouldn't be good.

Still, he'd decided what he wanted and what he wanted he got. Also, he hadn't seen the inside of Lark's little flat, but he'd seen the outside and while it seemed decent enough, if small, it wasn't a suitable place for his child to grow up in. There was no garden for a start, nowhere for a little girl to run around in and play.

And you know all about how a child should grow up?

He knew enough. A child shouldn't grow up in the shadow of his parents' brutal war of a marriage. A pawn to be used to punish and undermine each other. A weapon to be used in a war caused by love turned into toxic obsession.

It was his father Giovanni's cheating that had started it. Cesare had been about five then, and his mother, Bianca, had then demanded a divorce after she'd found out. But Giovanni had refused. He wouldn't be the first Donati in history to divorce and anyway, Bianca had to stay and care for her child. Cesare needed a mother.

Bianca had been furious, but she'd stayed and things had been all right for a little while. Back then Cesare had loved his mother and had tried to be good for her in case his behaviour set off one of her rapid mood swings. She'd told him he was her good boy, her most loving son. That they needed to leave, to escape his father, who didn't love him the way she loved him. He'd believed her and so when she'd packed him a bag and held out a hand, he'd taken it and together they'd escaped.

It had seemed an exciting adventure, a chance to be with his lovely mother who'd sworn she'd protect him from his terrible father.

Then Giovanni had caught up with them, and he'd been furious. He'd dragged Cesare away by force, while his mother had screamed in rage, and taken him back to the palazzo. The next day Giovanni had told his son that he'd been worried for him, afraid for his safety, because his mother was sick. That she'd lied to him, that she didn't care about him. But Giovanni did. He loved Cesare. He was his heir after all. Oh, and he wasn't allowed to see Bianca again.

If Bianca had known what was good for her, she should have left then, but she couldn't stand that Giovanni had won this particular battle. Forgiveness had never been part of her makeup and so she'd stayed at the palazzo, living in a separate wing like a ghost, haunting her husband every chance she got.

She would leave little notes around the palazzo for Cesare, telling him that she was staying there for him, that she could never leave him, that Giovanni was intent on punishing her by keeping Cesare from her. But they couldn't let him win, she'd said. Cesare should be ready, because one day she would come for him and they'd finally leave for good.

Giovanni found one of the notes and told Cesare furiously that he was to burn them. That his mother was only telling him these things to hurt him, that the only thing she cared about was punishing Giovanni.

His father had been a proud man, arrogant and stiff-necked, and rigid. And he'd expected his son to be the same, and Cesare had tried. He'd hated the fight between his parents and he'd thought that if he was good enough for both of them, then somehow this terrible war would finally end.

But it didn't. It only escalated.

Giovanni tried to get Bianca removed from the house, but she refused to go. One day she turned up after one of Cesare's riding lessons at the stables, and he'd been so pleased to see her. When she said she'd brought them a little picnic, he'd gone with her without hesitation.

She'd taken him to one of his favourite spots on the grassy bank beside the river that ran through the palazzo's ground, and poured him a cup of some special drink she had in a thermos. 'Drink it all, my darling,' she'd told him, drinking some herself. 'Drink it all and you can be with Mama for ever and ever.'

There had been a feverish light in her eyes and she'd seemed jumpy and tense, but he'd wanted to be a good boy for her, so he'd swallowed the whole cup. Then the world seemed to spin and he'd started feeling horribly sick.

His last memories of that day were of lying on the blanket Bianca had laid out and hearing his father's voice shouting angrily and his mother screaming back.

Then he'd blacked out and woken in hospital, where doctors stood around his bed, looking grim. He'd had no idea what happened, other than that he'd been very sick, and still was.

A day later, a stern-looking woman had appeared at his bedside. She was his aunt and she was there to look after him, because his parents had died.

Later, he'd found out that his mother had tried to poison him and herself that day beside the river, because she'd wanted to punish his father once and for all. The only reason he was alive was due to his father discovering that Bianca had taken him from his riding lesson and so he'd gone to find her. No one knew exactly what had happened then, but the facts were that his mother had died from a gunshot wound and his father the same.

The theory was, he'd killed her before shooting himself.

He certainly hadn't cared that his son had been poisoned and only saved by one of the stable hands who'd come to investigate the gunshots.

They'd told him they cared about him, that they loved him, but he knew then that his only importance was as a way to hurt each other. That no matter how good a son he'd been to both of them, hoping it would help them, it hadn't. Nothing he'd done had mattered at all. And if that was the case, then what was the point of being good? Of caring about other people, when no one had cared about him?

No, he had only himself to answer to and why not? Why not accept the legacy his parents had left him? They were dead and gone, leaving him alone, and so why shouldn't he rip his father's precious legacy apart? Erase the memory of his mother?

That the best thing he could do with a family like his

was to raze it then salt the earth, so that nothing ever grew from its poisoned soil again.

Except now there was Maya, who wasn't poisonous or toxic. Who'd been brought up by a mother who'd loved her and that was all she'd ever known. It had to stay that way.

'Cesare?' Aristophanes asked in bored tones. 'You've been quiet for an awfully long time. What were you saying about the mother?'

A jolt went through him. Why was he thinking about his parents? They had nothing to do with this.

'Maya's mother will not be pleased,' he said, trying to get his thoughts back in order. 'But I'm sure we can work something out.'

'Take her to bed,' Aristophanes said. 'I'm sure that will make her more conducive. Either that or offer to marry her.'

Cesare scowled. 'I assume you know why marriage is the last thing I would offer?'

Aristophanes, who knew Cesare's past, only sighed as if the topic was of the most utter disinterest to him. 'It would give her some legal protection and also money, which I'm sure she'd like. Also, I'm sure you'd like Maya to have your name.'

Cesare came to halt in the middle of his study, thinking.

He hadn't thought about marriage. Why would he? Marriage had never been something he wanted, not after the battleground it had become for his parents. Marriage seemed like a glass case, a trap where two people who couldn't get out turned on each other and destroyed each other, not caring if they took other people down with them.

'I didn't know you cared about my name,' Cesare growled.

'I don't, but you do. You being a Donati and all.' Aristophanes was a self-made man and had a healthy disdain for such things as family history and legacy. He'd long told Cesare that it was his considerable financial acumen that Aristophanes respected, not his name, and certainly not his history.

Cesare couldn't blame him. He didn't respect his own history either.

Still, now that Aristophanes had mentioned marriage, he couldn't let go of the idea. Marriage to Lark… There would be benefits to it, he had to admit. She'd obviously live with him and that would be useful. Maya should have her mother close and if Lark lived at the palazzo with him then they wouldn't need any messy custody arrangements. Also, yes, then Maya would take his name and legally be a Donati.

If he really thought about it, it wasn't marriage that was the trap, it was love. Love that could turn to hate in the blink of an eye, love that could make people do the most terrible things. He wanted nothing whatsoever to do with love. The good thing about his relationship with Lark was that he didn't love her. She certainly didn't love him, which meant they'd be spared that hideousness. Of course there was the issue of sex and how that would work between them since she'd told him she wasn't going to sleep with him again. Perhaps marriage might change her mind?

Then again, if it didn't, it was no problem. They could each have discreet lovers.

Really? You're saying you wouldn't mind Lark having a lover?

Something hot tightened in his gut at the thought, but he shoved it away before he could name it. Lark could have a lover. It wouldn't be an issue.

'Perhaps,' he said. 'It is important that Maya be a Donati.'

'I thought as much.' Aristophanes was clearly not interested in further discussion. 'Well, it's your funeral, my friend. Let me know when the happy occasion is and I'll make sure I have time in my schedule.'

Aristophanes lived or died by his schedule, Cesare knew. If it wasn't in the schedule it didn't happen. 'Of course,' he said. 'I'll let you know as soon as I have a date.'

He disconnected the call and then paced around a bit more, going over a myriad of plans.

Then the door opened and one of his assistants came in with the results of the test.

It was as he'd thought. Maya was his child.

He stared down at the piece of paper and the satisfaction that had settled down inside him became solid rock. There would be no more argument. No more discussion. Maya was a Donati and she would be raised one. She would be his hope for the future, a new generation rising out of the ashes of the old, and he had the opportunity to provide a better legacy for her than what his parents had left for him.

Are you sure she's not better off without you? Your parents certainly would have been.

The voice in his head was snide, taunting, but he shoved it away before the doubt had time to take root. No, she wasn't better off. She was heir to a difficult history and someone needed to help her come to terms with it. Someone would also need to teach her how to deal with her considerable inheritance, and he was the best person to do that.

He was her father, and although he didn't know how to be a good one, he'd certainly had experience of a bad one. He'd never be like his own father, never ever.

Cesare left his study and went down the stairs to the front room, pausing in the doorway.

Lark was on her knees next to Maya, both of them playing with the large plastic truck he'd bought. Lark was pretending to drive it around while Maya squealed with delight as she tried to grab it. And a peculiar sensation caught at him as he watched them.

His daughter playing with her mother, full of laughter and joy. Lark smiling at her child, her face shining. They were both enjoying themselves, clearly happy.

He'd never had that, he realised. Not in his own life. His childhood had been nothing but tension and hatred, a cold war with him in the middle. His childhood had been stolen from him by his parents and he wouldn't do the same to Maya.

His child would have a different childhood. He would give her joy and laughter and happiness, and he knew that the best way to do that was to make sure Lark was at his side.

That wasn't just important. That was vital.

Sensing his presence, Lark looked up, her pretty green

eyes locking with his. She went still. Maya, taking no notice of her parents, grabbed at the truck, babbling happily.

'Oh,' Lark breathed, searching his face. 'So…it's true then?'

He didn't move. 'Yes. Do you want to see the results for yourself?'

A complicated expression passed over her features. All the happiness disappeared, leaving disappointment, he thought, and fear, and also despair. She looked away sharply, hiding it from him. 'No,' she said in a curiously blank voice. 'I believe you.'

Cesare did not bother himself with other people's emotions or opinions. He didn't care about them, not a single iota. But he didn't like that expression on Lark's face. Not the disappointment or despair, and definitely *not* the fear. That wasn't what he wanted for her and he didn't want that for Maya either.

Lark's happiness was vital to his daughter's, he could see that now, which meant it was now going to be vital to him.

'We need to talk, little bird,' Cesare said quietly.

CHAPTER SEVEN

LARK TOOK A deep breath. She'd known this moment was coming, that she had to stop denying what she already knew. And she did know, even before she'd seen the look on his face as he'd stood in that doorway watching her and Maya.

Cesare *was* Maya's father and she had to accept it. She had to accept, too, that he wanted to be in Maya's life. He'd never made any secret of that.

She couldn't change it, just as she couldn't change that he was the father of her child, but that didn't mean she didn't have any choices or any power. In fact, she knew exactly what kind of power she had and while she'd waited for the results of that test, her brain running through various scenarios, she knew what choice she was going to make too.

She didn't have the resources to fight a man like him, and she wasn't going to run like her mother. Cesare was a man who knew what he wanted and she suspected that even if she did run, she wouldn't get far.

But she didn't want to run. She wanted her daughter to be happy. To grow up without fear, to have a home where she could put down roots and be safe. To be loved.

Cesare would no doubt insist on Maya living with

him and Lark couldn't protest. He had a beautiful house with beautiful gardens, plenty of room for Maya to run around and play in. She'd grow up there, have a life there. She'd have everything she ever needed and Lark couldn't deny her that.

But she wasn't going to let Cesare take Maya without her. Where Maya went, so would Lark, and if he was going to take her to Italy, then he'd have to put up with Lark coming too.

He might protest, but there were ways she could make it attractive to him. Her body for example, could be a powerful inducement.

For Maya's sake.

Not for your own?

She caught her breath, a wave of heat washing over her.

Cesare had hitched a shoulder against the doorframe, his blue gaze fixed on her. He'd taken his jacket off and got rid of his banana-stained tie, so he was in his shirt-sleeves. He'd rolled up the cuffs, strong forearms exposed, hands in the pockets of his suit trousers and there was something so incredibly sexy about them, about him leaning there casually, watching her…

She couldn't keep lying to herself. She couldn't keep pretending that she didn't want him. Couldn't keep telling herself that once had been enough and that all her curiosity had been satisfied, because it wasn't. How could she keep going forward when he was here? Reminding her of that night and of everything she'd forgotten?

Something had happened between them that night in Rome, something special and not only the conception of her daughter. Something else. Something that had kept him wanting her even though two years had passed. And she'd missed out on it.

It hadn't been just sex either, she felt it in her bones. It had been something else, something more, something that made her ache with a loss she didn't understand. Didn't she owe it to herself to find out what it had been? Who *he* had been to her and she to him?

She wouldn't find that out by continuing to deny herself, that was for certain.

'Okay,' she said, getting to her feet. 'Let's talk.'

Cesare pushed himself away from the doorframe. 'Not here. Up in my study.' He turned and made a gesture and Emily, the nanny who'd been looking after Maya while Lark had been in Rome, stepped through the doorway and into the room.

Of course, Lark thought with a hint of wry amusement. He'd thought of everything. Even making sure that Maya had someone familiar looking after her.

As Emily settled in, Lark gave Maya a kiss then followed Cesare out of the room and up the stairs. He went down a hallway, opened a dark oak door, and showed her into the large room beyond. Then he came in after her, shutting the door behind him.

'Please, sit.' He gestured to the chair that stood in front of his desk.

It wasn't an order. It was a request, so Lark did, settling herself in the chair. She expected him to go around the desk and sit in the chair behind it, but he didn't.

Instead, he came over to the desk and leaned back against it, folding his arms and looking down at her. He was very close, the warmth of his body and his scent making her mouth go dry.

She really had to get it together. He was going to start making proclamations and demands, she was sure, and she couldn't let him. Because once he started doing that, she'd be left carrying along in his wake, and she couldn't afford that. Not when she had demands of her own.

'I know what you want,' she said determinedly, before he could speak. 'You want to take Maya to live with you in Italy. At your palazzo presumably. And you want to bring her up as a Donati.'

Cesare opened his mouth, but she held up a hand. 'Let me finish please.'

He shut it.

'I can't fight you on this,' she went on. 'I don't have the resources, the connections or the power, and to be honest, it's better for Maya if I don't fight you. I know what it's like when parents are fighting each other and it's always the children that get caught in the middle.'

A strange expression crossed his face at that, but he didn't speak.

'I also know that Maya will have much better opportunities if she lives with you. She'll have room to run and play, she'll be safe. She'll have a home of her own rather than a rented flat and a mother struggling to make ends meet.'

Cesare opened his mouth again, but Lark shook a finger at him. 'I haven't finished.'

He shut it, but this time there was a glint of amusement in his eyes. She didn't trust it, but there wasn't anything else to do but go on. 'So, I'll agree that you should take her back to Italy to live, on one condition.' She stared at him fiercely. 'There will be no negotiation on this and I won't accept anything less. And if you want to honour the promise you made to me that you wouldn't take her away from me, you'll agree to this.'

He still looked amused, damn him, but all he did was make a *go on* gesture.

Lark took a breath. 'I will be coming too. Now, I don't care what you think of that or of how you'll find accommodation for me, but that'll be your problem. I will be coming with Maya because I'm her mother and she needs me. I won't accept separate accommodation from her and I will absolutely not be paying you any money for rent or board or—'

'Lark,' Cesare interrupted finally, his mouth curving. 'Will you allow me a word?'

'If you're going to tell me that you're not—'

'Lark,' he repeated, more gently this time. 'I agree.'

All the justifications and reasons she'd prepared about why he had to accept her offer flew abruptly out of her head. She gaped at him. 'You what?'

'I agree,' he said again. 'You're right. I do want to take her to Italy and bring her up as a Donati at the palazzo. And you're also right that she needs you at her side. A fight is the last thing I want between us, and I've already been planning to bring you with me to Rome. You will live at the Donati palazzo too and of course I won't demand any money from you.'

She'd been expecting to fight, to have to dig in her heels, and for a moment Lark couldn't think of a word to say.

'You…you won't?' she said at last.

'No.' He shifted against the desk and this time the glitter in his eyes wasn't only amusement, but something else. Something hotter. 'However, I do have a demand of my own.'

A thread of what felt suspiciously like anticipation coiled inside her, as if she was excited by the thought of whatever he was going to demand of her.

You like fighting him as much as he likes fighting you.

Of course, she did. The freedom she had with him to be angry was something she'd never had before, and yes, she liked it. Very much.

She caught her breath, trying to ignore the delicious shiver that crept over her skin. 'Oh? And what's that?'

Cesare smiled. 'I want you to marry me.'

Shock wound through her. That was…not what she'd expected him to ask. 'You want me to marry you?' she repeated stupidly.

'Sì.' More amusement glittered in Cesare's blue gaze, yet there was also the steel in it. This was something he would not be moved on. 'You're Maya's mother and I'm her father, and I think the whole thing would work best if we were married.'

'But…you can't *want* to marry me.'

'Not in the traditional sense, no,' he agreed, and why that should catch at her like a thorn, she had no idea. 'But in a legal sense I think it's absolutely necessary. Maya would have my name and so would you, which would give you resources and protection in case anything should happen to me.'

Lark felt her mouth go dry. Marriage had never been something she'd wanted for herself, not after witnessing the aftermath of her mother's experience. Her father had been abusive, Grace had told her, and yet there were some days when her mother refused to get out of bed and no amount of Lark's smiles would help. Where Grace would sit there slowly turning the wedding ring she still wore around and around on her finger, and staring at it. Grace had always told her she'd been glad to leave, that she'd had to in order to protect Lark and herself, but those days Lark would wonder if Grace was really as glad as she made out. If there was a part of her mother who still loved her father and missed him, no matter what he'd done to her.

That thought had horrified Lark, and she'd decided then and there that she'd never get married. Never allow herself to be trapped by a man. Never fall in love.

Yet now, here she was, looking down the barrel of a marriage proposal and… Well. She wasn't in love with Cesare Donati—a small mercy—but she was actually contemplating marrying him. He was by his own admission a selfish man, arrogant and proud, and there was no way she should even be thinking about tying herself to him, and yet….

He'd kept his word about not taking Maya from her when he easily could have and he clearly believed that his daughter needed her mother. He was also serious about protecting her and putting her needs before his own, despite confessing how he hadn't wanted children.

The addition of a daughter wasn't going to make his life simpler and if he truly hadn't wanted her, he'd had plenty of opportunity to walk away. In fact, Lark had encouraged him to do so. But he hadn't. And now not only had he not protested at the idea of having another person come to live with him, he was also offering her his name. For Maya's sake.

'I...' she began, her voice husky. 'I...will need some assurances.'

One inky brow rose. 'Another agreement perhaps?'

'Um...yes.' She folded her hands in her lap to stop them shaking.

'You would have complete freedom,' Cesare said, watching her in that intense way he had. 'I understand what you'll be giving up to come to Italy, so I can use my connections to help you find another job or assist you into study if that's what you prefer. Or if you'd rather be a full-time mother to Maya then I will support you. You'll want for nothing.'

Lark's head spun. She'd never thought seriously about what she'd wanted for herself. Before Maya had come along, she'd had thoughts of going to university and had been looking into bridging courses since her constant moving around with her mother had meant patchy schooling. She'd never got university entrance. Then once she'd moved to London, and after a year or so of bouncing between temping jobs, she'd found out she was pregnant and all thoughts of university had been put on the back burner.

Taking up Cesare's offer meant that she'd finally have the time to think about university and what she wanted for herself, because Maya would be taken care of.

Don't get ahead of yourself. He's a businessman through and through, and he'll want something in return.

That was true. He *would* want something in return and she could well imagine what that might be.

Lark was conscious that her palms were damp and her heart was racing, but she forced herself to meet his gaze head-on. 'But presumably *you'll* want something,' she said.

'I will?'

'Yes, in return for agreeing to marry you.'

The hot gleam in his eyes became even hotter. 'Why? Is there something you want to give me?'

'Don't play games with me, Cesare,' she said, nerves getting the better of her. 'Not about this. You know what I'm talking about.'

He gave her a slow burning smile. 'If it's sex you mean, then no, I will not require sex from you. In fact, I won't require anything of you.'

Something tightened in her gut and she couldn't tell if it was relief or disappointment.

'Unless you want to exercise your conjugal rights of course,' Cesare went on. 'In which case I'll be happy to assist you. But failing that, since I have no intention of being celibate, I will be taking lovers. Discreetly of course, and I expect that you'll want to do the same.'

She swallowed. It was definitely relief, wasn't it? 'You mean be discreet if I want a lover myself?'

'Yes. You needn't stay celibate on my account.'

Except the thought of having lovers herself left her cold.

You only want him.

She ignored that thought too. 'And if it doesn't work out? There'll be an option for divorce?'

A shadow flickered through Cesare's eyes. 'You want an escape clause?'

'Yes.' There was no point pretending. 'Don't you? You

might meet someone else, for example, and fall in love and want to marry them instead.'

'Oh, that will never happen.' There was an unexpected edge in his voice. 'Love is for other people, little bird. Not for me.'

He said the word *love* with a certain distaste, as if it was poison and it caught at her, waking a curiosity she hadn't known she'd felt until now. He'd sounded so very emphatic and she found herself wondering why. What was love to him? Had he been disappointed by it? Hurt by it?

Again, she was reminded that he knew things about her yet she didn't know about him. Personal things. She'd told him about her mother, about her past, but had he told her about his? Had he mentioned anything about himself that night?

You'll have time to find out now, won't you?

Deep inside her, the anticipation that had gathered before turned slowly into a hot, tense excitement. Marrying Cesare Donati could prove to be interesting, very interesting, and she couldn't deny that it affected her in a way she hadn't expected.

'Well, little bird?' The look on his face was intense, as if her answer mattered to him. 'What do you say? Will you accept my proposal?'

The inexplicable, mysterious excitement pulled tight, making her breathless. Perhaps it wouldn't be a bad idea to say yes, to marry him. Perhaps it didn't need to be just for Maya's sake either. After all, how long had it been since she'd done anything for herself? How long since she'd had a place to call her own? A place to stay and put down roots. A home. She had her flat, it was true, and her job, but the flat wasn't hers and while she'd liked working for Mr Ravenswood and he'd been training her, it wasn't exactly a career.

She'd never have the money to buy her own place, not on her own, and having to provide for Maya meant study was out of the question too.

But all that would change if she married Cesare.

Was it even a choice?

'Is that really how you're going to propose to me?' she said, unable to resist the urge to poke at him just a little, to get revenge for him surprising her like this. 'Standing up like that with your arms folded?'

Blue flames leapt in his eyes, the heat intensifying. 'How else would you like me to propose to you?'

His voice was deep with a sensual edge she found unbelievably sexy.

Lark held his gaze. 'Surely on one knee.'

Cesare's beautiful mouth curved and for a second she wasn't sure if he'd do it. Then abruptly he pushed himself away from the desk, standing in front of her. Then he leaned down and put both hands on the arms of her chair. He didn't let go as he lowered himself fluidly to the floor, on one knee as she'd instructed.

'Lark Edwards,' he said formally. 'Will you do me the honour of becoming my wife?'

Lark's pretty face was flushed, her green eyes glowing with a mixture of challenge and heat, and although he'd never taken kindly to being told what to do, he'd found himself going down on one knee all the same.

He could never resist a challenge and he could resist one from her even less.

Especially when he had an ulterior motive.

She'd surprised him, he couldn't deny it. He'd been all ready to launch into a detailed explanation about how she needed to marry him and why, expecting her to argue with him. Vociferously. However, then she'd taken the wind out of his sails by telling him she was coming to Italy with Maya whether he liked it or not.

It hadn't been what he'd anticipated at all, which had delighted him.

In fact, as she'd sat there primly in the chair, her hands folded, resplendent in a pretty green dress and telling him in no uncertain terms what she wanted now she knew he was Maya's father, he'd been delighted with her full stop.

She was beautiful for a start, and then she'd been very clear she didn't want to argue with him because of Maya, which had earned his fierce agreement. She wouldn't put her issues before those of her child's and he agreed fiercely with that too.

It wasn't a small thing she was giving up for Maya's sake. Her job and her life here in London, and any plans she'd made for the future. But she hadn't argued and she hadn't protested. She'd agreed it was in Maya's best interests and was prepared to back that up with action.

Really, his child couldn't have had a better mother.

But it hadn't been until he'd actually asked her to be his wife that he'd realised how much he wanted her to say yes. And badly. In fact, it had been quite disturbing how much he wanted it. Disturbing too to realise that though he could force her to say yes, he didn't want to. He wanted it to be her choice, the way it had been her choice that night two years ago.

Yet the real issue with wanting it to be her choice was

that he had no control over her answer. As a man used to having control in all things, he did not like that at all, not one bit. However, he was also a man who knew how to turn things to his advantage so he was definitely going to do what he could to weight her choice in his favour.

She looked at him where he knelt on the floor in front her, and he was pleased to see surprise in her sea-green eyes. Clearly she hadn't expected him to kneel. But surprise wasn't the only thing in her gaze. He could see the flickers of sensual awareness there too, the embers of desire starting to glow.

He was still holding on to the arms of her chair, his body leaning lightly against her knees, making it impossible for her to ignore him physically. She was so small they were at eye level.

Pretty, pretty woman. She smelled so good. It was an aphrodisiac all on its own, and he could feel himself getting hard. He'd told her she'd look pretty on her knees, yet he was the one kneeling. Begging too, and not even for sex but for her name on a piece of paper.

He wanted her to say yes and not just for Maya's sake, but for his too.

His gaze held hers, the tension between them deepening the longer she stayed silent, the air around them becoming charged and crackling with static.

Cesare didn't look away as he let go the arms of the chair, putting his hands gently on either side of her thighs, just above her knees, and clasping her gently.

She gave a delicious little shiver but didn't pull away. 'I thought you weren't going to touch me again unless I asked?'

'I wasn't,' he admitted. 'But you haven't given me an answer yet and I thought I might offer some incentive.'

Lark's gaze drifted to his mouth, her gaze gone smoky. 'What incentive?'

'This.' He began to slowly ease up the hem of her dress, up the front of her calves and slowly over her knees, baring her pretty thighs. 'Our marriage doesn't have to be only about Maya. You could have something for yourself too. After all, don't you think you deserve it?'

'Do I?' She made no move to stop him, only staring at him, her breathing getting faster and faster as he pushed her dress even higher.

She hadn't asked for reassurance, and yet he found himself wanting to give it. Wanting her to understand too, that he was grateful for what she'd done for Maya. Because there were many choices she could have made when she'd found herself pregnant with a baby she had no memory of conceiving, and she'd chosen to keep her.

A difficult choice for a woman on her own, and he regretted that he hadn't been there to support her, to be with her when Maya was born. There was so much he'd missed. But one thing he knew was that this strong, beautiful woman had kept their daughter safe, had kept her happy and healthy and, yes, for that he was grateful.

'Yes,' he murmured. 'Of course you do.' He eased the hem of her dress up to her waist so he could see the knickers she wore, white cotton with a bit of lace. Very practical. Incredibly sexy. 'You kept her when you could have chosen differently, and that must have been very hard.' He slid his hands up her thighs, stroking her silky skin and she took a soft breath. 'Especially having to do this all on your own.'

Lark's gaze became liquid, her full lower lip trembling slightly. 'I wanted so badly to be a good mother to her,' she whispered. 'But sometimes…'

'It's okay.' He stroked her slowly, hoping she saw his sincerity, because he'd never been so sincere in all his life. 'I'm sorry I wasn't there to help you. But I am now, understand? You've done a fantastic job with her, but you're not alone in this any more.'

Her throat moved, and she stared at him as if she was drowning and his gaze was a lifeline. He could smell her vanilla scent, tinged now with the delicate musk of her arousal, and something primitive and powerful turned over inside him.

She needed him, he could see that now, it was there in her eyes, and he liked it. He'd never been needed before, not like this, and it made him want to be there for her, protect her the way she'd protected their daughter.

He would get that yes from her. She would be his wife. She and Maya were his now and it was his responsibility to keep them both safe and happy.

And touching her now wasn't only about weighting the dice in his favour. It was also a token of his gratitude for what she'd done for their daughter, and his appreciation for her strength and courage. Pleasure, just for her and her alone.

Cesare looked into her eyes, seeing the flickers of her passion beginning to ignite, and he bent his head, brushing his mouth over the top of one thigh and then the other.

Her breath hitched, yet she made no move to stop him. So he reached up and hooked his fingers in the waistband of her knickers and slowly drew them down. She sighed, lifting up to help him, then leaning back in the chair as he pulled them all the way off and dropped them on the floor.

Then he leaned in again and gently eased her thighs apart.

'Cesare…' she whispered, shivering.

'Little bird.' His thumbs stroked over her skin as he glanced hungrily at the soft golden curls between her thighs. *Dio*, she was gorgeous. Then he met her gaze once again. 'You are so beautiful. So strong and brave. Our little girl is healthy and happy, and that is all down to you. I want to show you how much that means to me, give you the pleasure you deserve. And I won't lie… I also want to show you what you could have as my wife, what a good husband can give you.'

Her eyes had gone dark with arousal, her face flushed. 'Yes. Yes, please…'

His own hunger was becoming demanding and he was hard, but for once in his life Cesare wasn't interested in his own pleasure. The only thing that mattered was hers.

He bent, nuzzling gently at her inner thighs, pressing kisses there as he went, hearing her breathing get faster and faster. He remembered how she'd tasted that night, remembered her cries of delight as he'd brought her to the edge of orgasm and held her there. That memory had lived in his head for so long and he'd never thought he'd ever get the chance to taste her again.

Yet here she was, between his hands and he couldn't wait.

He was so damn hungry.

He gripped her thighs and leaned in, nuzzling against

the soft curls and kissing her there. Then he tightened his grip and using his tongue, began to explore the soft, damp folds of her sex.

Lark cried out, moving restlessly in his hands, but he didn't let go. He leaned in further, exploring her deeper, wanting to drive her to the edge of sanity and hold her there for as long as possible.

She was delicious. He wanted to do this all day, have her shaking and trembling and crying out as he gave her all the pleasure she deserved and then some.

His groin ached, his own need becoming demanding, but he shoved it aside. It wasn't important, not right now, not compared to her.

He knew how to pleasure a woman, knew how to bring her to the brink and hold her there. Knew how to use his hands and his mouth to give her the greatest ecstasy, and he did so now. Kissing her, licking, feasting on her. Devouring her as if she was the most delicious treat he'd ever tasted and she was.

She twisted in the chair and he felt her fingers in his hair, clutching at him as he continued to tease and to lick and to nip, using his fingers and then his tongue, circling and stroking that most sensitive part of her.

And he finally got what he wanted, her begging at the end, her fingers knotted in his hair, twisting in his grip as she tried to get that final friction that would send her over the edge.

But he denied her and denied her, wringing as much pleasure from her as he could until finally, with a light flick of his tongue, he gave her what she needed most.

Lark screamed, her body convulsing as the orgasm swept her, and he tasted it, salty and sweet and addictive. Then he held her in his hands as she sobbed and trembled through the aftershocks, and only once she'd quietened did he ease back, looking at her.

Her head had lolled against the back of the chair, her eyes shut and her mouth slightly open, the gleam of perspiration at her throat.

He waited a moment then dealt with her clothes, calmly pulling her dress back down and covering her, while she watched him from beneath long, golden lashes.

'What about you?' she asked eventually, her voice hoarse. 'Don't you want—?'

'No,' he interrupted gently. 'That was for you. I don't need anything in return.'

She stared at him a long moment. 'You want me to say yes, don't you?'

He could tell her it didn't matter, not let her know how much he wanted it, but he couldn't lie, not to her. Not now.

So all he said was, 'I do. Very much.'

She was silent a long time, just looking at him. Then she said unexpectedly, 'I don't want another lover, Cesare. I want you. I want this.'

There was triumph inside him and a wave of satisfaction so intense it should have been a warning sign. But if so, it was a warning he paid no attention to, because he wanted more of this too.

'Then what is your answer, little bird?'

'Yes,' she said softly. 'My answer is yes.'

CHAPTER EIGHT

THINGS MOVED VERY quickly after Lark had agreed to be his wife. Cesare Donati was a man who apparently didn't let any grass grow under his feet.

He gave her some time to collect her and Maya's most important items from her flat, and to hand in her notice to Mr Ravenswood, then a week or so later, Lark found herself on a jet back to Italy.

Mr Ravenswood hadn't been too happy to lose her, though he'd been even more unhappy at losing the antiques since Cesare was now not going to sell them. However, he was mollified by Cesare promising to use his connections when it came to sourcing other items, and soon gave Lark a glowing reference.

Cesare had also organised for his staff to pack up her flat and clean it, which was a relief since she didn't relish having to do it herself.

As far as the whole marriage thing went, Cesare had asked her what she preferred in terms of a ceremony since he didn't much care, though he did warn her that since he was quite a public figure, media interest would be high. But she didn't want to make a big deal of it since it wasn't as if theirs was a love match and told him so.

He didn't waste any time with that either and as soon

as they'd landed, Emily was sent to the palazzo with Maya, while Lark found herself having an impromptu wedding ceremony in a tiny chapel near the airport.

Afterwards, she sat in the limo staring at the rose-gold ring on her finger as she and Cesare drove to the palazzo. Somehow he'd found the time to get her the most beautiful ring. It was inset with tiny emeralds and was actually very beautiful.

She could hardly believe it. She was Signora Donati now and Maya had a little family. Perhaps she should have felt afraid or even had a hint of foreboding, but she didn't.

This had been the right thing to do, she knew it.

Of course, what life would be like now she was Cesare's wife was another story, as was what kind of marriage they'd have once they were settled.

He'd been true to his word and had had another agreement drawn up, and this time he'd had a third party look over it for her. There had been nothing in it to cause alarm. He hadn't even bothered with a prenup about his wealth in the event of a divorce. There had only been mention of custody arrangements for Maya and a certain amount of money for her upkeep too.

Lark had signed the agreement without protest, though she still felt a degree of uncertainty.

She couldn't stop thinking about the day he'd asked her to be his wife, and how he'd knelt before her chair, his hands stroking her, telling her that she was strong and beautiful, and that she'd been an excellent mother for Maya. And that she wasn't alone any more.

The sincerity with which he'd said it, so totally unexpected, had made her heart clench tight in her chest and unexpected tears rise. She had no idea how he'd known about the doubts she'd buried so far down she'd forgotten they were there. Doubts about the kind of mother she was, and whether she'd made the right choice in bringing Maya up by herself. They were always there, those doubts, and somehow Cesare had seen them, had brought them to the light, and then had looked into her eyes and told her that yes, she'd made the right choice. That he was glad she had, and that Maya was happy and healthy and that was the important thing. That she'd done a good job and he appreciated it.

He appreciated her.

Then he'd given her the most intense pleasure, taking her quickly and skilfully apart with the touch of his mouth and hands. He'd told her she was beautiful and brave and then he made her feel both of those things. He'd told her she wasn't alone and for the first time in her life, she actually felt it. Even as a child, loneliness had stalked her, because although she'd had her mother, it had never seemed as if Grace was really there. She was either in the depths of a depression, or staring off in the distance, turning that ring on her finger, gone somewhere in her thoughts that Lark couldn't follow. Her mother's attention had seemed a fleeting thing. There and then gone again in the blink of an eye, even though she was physically present.

But Cesare had knelt at her feet and looked at her, seeing her. Focusing all his intense attention on her, and she'd felt the weight of that attention settle on her. It wasn't heavy though, only deeply reassuring on a level she couldn't describe.

He meant it though, she'd seen it. Every word he'd said to her that day, he'd meant.

And now he was her husband; she didn't have any desire to go searching for a lover. She'd half thought, before he'd got down on his knees and made her feel so unbelievably good, that perhaps she wouldn't mind being celibate, since it had never bothered her before.

But he'd shown her the error of that particular piece of thinking, and in addition to reassuring her doubts, he'd somehow awakened the passion inside her, until she hadn't been able to think of anything else but him. Of what it would be like to be in a bed, naked, with him. Of how good it would be and how starved she'd been for physical touch.

As they pulled up to the palazzo, her new home, Lark made a decision. They hadn't discussed what kind of marriage they were going to have in the days leading up to it, such as whether they'd share a room and sleep together every night, or whether she'd have her own.

But she knew what she wanted. Sharing a room, sharing a bed.

He might not like that, but she was going to ask for it nonetheless.

Cesare got out of the limo, opened the door for her. 'Emily will be looking after Maya all afternoon,' he said as she stepped out onto the gravel, the blue of his eyes burning fiercely. 'I organised specially so you and I could have a wedding night.'

Emily had been looking after Maya on and off over the past few weeks, and Cesare had employed her to come to Italy with them since he wanted Maya to have someone familiar looking after her when her parents weren't able to.

Lark could feel her own desire start to rise in response to his, yet he must have picked up on some of her uncertainty, because he frowned all of a sudden. 'What is it?' he asked. 'Did you not want—'

'No,' she said quickly. 'No, it's not that. We just… haven't discussed anything about this marriage, Cesare. I mean, how it will work and what it will look like.'

'What is there to discuss? You'll be living here with me and Maya, and I'm hoping you feel the same way I do about sharing a bed.'

She swallowed and looked him in the eye. 'Every night? And it will be "our" bed, not just yours?'

'Yes.' He held her gaze. 'You will have your own space, but it will be "our" bed and "our" room.'

The last shred of tension left her and she let out a breath. 'Okay, so apart from the living arrangements and sex,' she said, as staff bustled around, taking luggage out of the car and into the house. 'I also don't know anything about you and I'd like to.'

He shut the limo door then paused. 'What do you want to know?'

'I told you all about my childhood and my past. About my mother and growing up on the run. You know about me, but I don't know anything about you. Unless you told me that night?' She looked up at him, part of her hoping that it hadn't only been her who'd opened her heart, that he too had reciprocated.

But slowly he shook his head. 'No. My past, my family history is…dark. And I didn't want to talk about it that night. You were so warm and open, and you needed someone to talk to. I didn't want to make it about me or drag you down into a discussion about my family's dramatics.'

The words sounded casual, but she heard it again, the slight edge. The edge that always carried in his voice whenever he spoke about his family.

It was something bad—she could see the shadows stealing through his gaze—and part of her wondered if now was a good time to talk about it, especially since they'd only just been married. Then again, maybe now was the perfect time, so she knew immediately what she and by extension Maya were getting into.

'Well, I'd like to know,' she said. 'I mean, shouldn't I know something about the man I married and the family I married into?'

'You are looking at the entirety of the family you married into.' His voice had gone curiously blank. 'I'm the last heir. Or at least I was until Maya appeared.'

She'd heard about that. It was what the media called him. Perhaps she should have done some internet research on her own about him, but she'd been too busy the past week with moving and getting things organised.

'Will you tell me about it?' she asked.

His blue gaze had gone dark. 'Are you sure you want to know? A quick internet search should tell you everything.'

'Maybe. But I'd rather not get Maya's family history from the internet. I'd prefer to hear it from her father.'

He was silent a moment. 'Well, don't say I didn't warn you.' He held out a hand. 'Come with me.'

She took it, his fingers threading through hers warm and strong, then followed him as he led her in through the palazzo's ornate entrance and into the huge salon where she'd first met him only a couple of weeks earlier. He let go of her hand, stopping before the fireplace and glancing up at the portrait hanging above it, of the stern-looking man and the pretty woman with rose-gold hair.

'Those are my parents,' he said. 'Giovanni and Bianca Donati. They married for love by all accounts, not that you'd know it in the end.' He put his hands in his pockets, still staring up at the portrait. 'I don't remember a time when they weren't fighting. My first memory was of them arguing about whether I should have a nanny or not. My father insisted that I should, while my mother insisted that I shouldn't, that I had her. Mama was intense about her opinions, hated to conform, harboured grudges and never admitted she was wrong, while my father was proud and rigid and fanatical about traditions. *Compromise* wasn't a word either of them understood. They spent an entire month arguing about it. Papa kept hiring nannies and Mama kept sending them away until she eventually got her way.'

Lark folded her arms, watching him.

'Then came my schooling. Papa wanted me to go to the boarding school he attended, Mama refused to let me go. She wanted to teach me herself. They argued about that on and off for six months, until eventually Papa hired tutors for me at home. That wasn't good enough for Mama and she continued to complain about it both to me and to Papa. She didn't like it when I was given riding lessons at six either. She thought I was too young and she and Papa had a shouting match about it. Papa won that round too.'

A sense of foreboding crept through Lark. This was not going to end well she could feel it.

'Papa had a business trip to London not long after that, and so my mother took me to America without telling him for a fun "holiday". He found out and was furious that she hadn't told him and that we went without security. She accused him of stifling me, he accused her of being lax and not putting my safety first, and so it continued. For some reason I became the thing they argued about almost constantly, and because they couldn't let anything go, it escalated.

I fell off my horse one day—it wasn't anything major—but Mama ordered my riding lessons to stop, and when Papa told her she was overreacting, it blew up into this huge screaming match. She demanded a divorce, but he refused, so she retaliated by waiting until he was on another business trip, then walking out and taking me with her.' Cesare's blue gaze came to hers and there was something in his blue eyes she didn't recognise. 'Donati staff found out and alerted Papa. He arrived at the airport in Rome just as we were about to go through security and he stopped us. Mama didn't care that we were in a public place, she screamed at him and he shouted back, while I was pulled between them.'

Lark's chest tightened. 'How old were you?'

'Eight.'

God. Eight and caught between shouting, screaming parents. She couldn't imagine how awful that must have been for him.

'Oh, Cesare,' she said softly.

'You think that's bad?' He smiled, but there was no amusement in it. 'Just wait. It gets worse. Papa took me home and refused to let her see me, telling her that he was happy for her to leave, but she wasn't taking me with her. Mama of course couldn't let that go. She always hated it when Papa won. So she told him the only way she was leaving was with me, and stayed. She camped out in one wing of the palazzo, arguing with him constantly, insisting that I be allowed to see her, that he was cruel to keep a mother from her child, etcetera, etcetera.' Cesare turned back to the portrait, his expression bitter. 'Eventually she wore him down and he allowed her supervised visits with me, but that only enraged her more. She didn't consider it a victory, telling me that he was a terrible father and didn't I want to be with her? That she loved me more than he ever would.'

Cesare paused a moment and she could see the tension in his tall figure, could feel it thread through her too, a crawling, aching dread.

'I was ten by then and one day she turned up for a scheduled visit after my riding class. We were going to have a picnic, she said, and somehow she managed to send the staff member who was supposed to be supervising us away. I hadn't seen her for about two weeks and I was…reluctant to go with her. She could never leave the subject of her grudge with Papa alone, and I always felt as if it was my fault somehow, especially since all they fought about was me. Anyway, that day she was…happy and seemed excited to see me, so I went on her picnic. We had it beside the river and there was delicious food. She poured me an orange juice from a thermos and gave it to me. Told me to drink the whole thing.'

His voice had become colder and Lark felt herself get colder too, the dread tightening.

'I started feeling dizzy and sick, and very sleepy, so I lay down, and she stroked my hair telling me that soon we'd be together and free of him. My last memory before I blacked out is of my father suddenly arriving and shouting, and her screaming back, and when I woke up, I was in hospital.'

Lark caught her breath in shock. 'What happened?'

Cesare glanced at her once again. 'Mama wanted to punish Papa once and for all and had poisoned the orange juice. Apparently she'd planned to poison me then herself. But the staff member she'd sent away went straight to Papa and he found us before she could drink the rest of the juice. He'd brought a gun and when he found out what she'd done, he shot her. Then he shot himself.'

Lark stared at him, horrified. She'd thought her childhood had been pretty bad, but that was nothing in comparison with his. That his own mother had tried to kill him and herself… Then his father shooting her…

'Cesare,' she began faintly yet again, only to stop, because she couldn't think of a word to say.

'Yes,' he said, the word full of bitterness. 'What kind of response can you to make to that? It's almost farcical in its dramatics, don't you think? But then that's the Donati family way. Our history is full people shooting, stabbing or poisoning people we don't like. It's a history of self-involvement. Of selfishness. Of putting our feelings ahead of anyone else's including our children's.' He gave a laugh that was utterly cold and cynical sounding. 'It wasn't exactly the world's most loving environment as you can imagine.'

Lark's mouth was dry, her chest tight. She felt almost crushed by the weight of a terrible sympathy for him, for a little boy caught between two self-involved individuals who'd cared more about their grudges than for their son.

At least her mother had cared. She'd escaped her marriage because she'd wanted to keep Lark safe.

Sure, but let her fear and paranoia make things difficult for you. You weren't allowed any bad feelings either, because it upset her.

Lark shoved the thought aside. That might be true, but if it hadn't been for Lark then her mother would never have had to run at all; she was not forgetting that.

Anyway, this wasn't about her. This was about Cesare.

She wanted to cross the room to where he stood and put her arms around him, give him some kind of comfort because it was the only thing she could think of to do.

It was a horrible story, a terrible one, and no child should ever have to experience their own parent trying to harm them the way he had. No child should ever have to think that it was their fault either, and from what he said, it was clear that part of him still blamed himself.

She took a step towards him, but he'd turned back to the painting, going over to the fireplace and putting his hands on the mantelpiece, staring up at the portrait. And there was something about his posture now, a subtle change in tension that kept her frozen where she was.

He didn't seem bitter now. He seemed furious.

'Anyway,' he went on. 'For years I ignored what they did to me. My aunt cared for me until I reached my majority, but she wasn't exactly a loving caregiver either. She died two years ago and it was then that I decided I was done with the Donati legacy. That I was going to burn it to the ground, break it up, sell everything and donate the proceeds to charity.'

Yet more shock echoed through her. 'What? All of it?'

'Yes.' He pushed himself away from the mantelpiece and turned to face her. 'Don't mistake me, little bird. I'm as selfish and self-serving as my parents. I tried to be good for them, to be the perfect son for them. I listened to my mother's complaints and I obeyed my father's every directive. I thought that if I was only good and obedient enough they'd finally stop arguing about me. But nothing I did made any difference, and for a long time I blamed myself for their deaths. They hadn't made a will, because they couldn't agree on the terms, at least that's what my aunt told me before she died, and that's when I realised the truth.

'Nothing I did made any difference to them, because they didn't care about me. Their arguments and grudges and petty slights were more important to them than providing for their child. So why should I care about them? Why should I blame myself for something that wasn't my fault? They were gone, but I still had their toxic legacy to look after and that's when I decided I was done looking after it.'

She didn't have an answer to that, mainly because she could understand why he felt that way. Who wouldn't? After they'd been treated the way he'd been treated?

'But you changed your mind about that, didn't you?' she asked.

'I did,' he agreed. 'I changed it the minute I saw Maya's picture on your phone and I knew she was mine.' His blue gaze gleamed suddenly. 'I decided she would be my new start. My new beginning. A chance to create a different Donati legacy, a better legacy. She's untouched by my history, by what my parents did to me, and I want her to stay untouched by it. I want her to grow up knowing what happiness is like, to put something better out in the world that isn't just selfishness.' He paused a moment. 'I want her to grow up to be a better person than I am, a better Donati.'

The tightness in Lark's chest wouldn't ease. He saw himself in such a negative light, didn't he? He called himself selfish, thought he wasn't a good person, though she didn't understand why. Then again, he'd grown up in the middle of a cold war, where the people who were supposed to protect him had been more interested in hurting each other. And they'd argued over him as if he was the problem, and he'd felt that way too. And she suspected that no matter what he'd told her about deciding he was done with blaming himself, a part of him still did. Why else would he keep seeing himself as selfish when everything he'd done so far was the opposite?

Well, however he felt, while she hated that he'd been forced into that position, she admired his resolution. Sometimes when she'd been younger, she'd often used to wonder what it would be like to just be allowed to be angry. To shout if you wanted to, cry if you wanted to. Not be told that your smile was the best thing about you and how great it was that you were always happy. How your positivity made the world a better place.

Then how your one bad mood could cause a depression spiral that ended with your mother not leaving her bed for days.

What would have happened if she'd been a little bit selfish herself?

But there was no point in thinking that. Her mother was gone and those kinds of thoughts were disloyal.

She'd been in a terrible situation and she'd done her best with Lark, so who was Lark to criticise?

'You're not a bad person, Cesare,' Lark said. 'Why demonise yourself? It was your parents who had the behavioural issues, not you.'

'I'm not demonising myself. I'm only accepting who I am. No one wins in a situation like that one and certainly not the child caught in the middle of it.'

'You're not selfish, though. Why would you think that?'

He lifted a shoulder. 'Because I want what I want when I want it. I wanted revenge for what my parents did to me, so I put it in motion. And then when I realised I had a child, I wanted to make sure she was the new legacy I put out in the world. It's not about her, Lark. It's about me and what I want. Don't ever forget that.'

But there was something in that statement that just didn't ring true, especially not after seeing him with Maya. And not after he'd knelt at her feet, the look on his face nothing but sincere as he told her she wasn't alone.

'You do care about her, though,' she said. 'You wanted me to come with her because she needed her mother and her happiness was important to you. And what you said to me—'

'It's the legacy, Lark,' he corrected her gently. 'That's all I care about. Creating a new and improved dynasty, that's all. Now.' The flame in his eyes leapt. 'I'm tired of talking about this. Why don't we get to our wedding night?'

There wasn't much distance between them and yet he felt suddenly as if any distance at all was far too much.

Nothing about his recitation of his terrible childhood should have been difficult, because it had been a very long time since he'd woken up in that hospital bed and his aunt had told him the truth about what happened.

Yet…he'd found himself tensing as he'd told Lark about it. Found that the fury he'd thought he'd buried, the fury that had consumed him as a teenager and that had no outlet because the people he was furious at were gone, was back. It simmered like a field of burning magma just under the earth's crust, scalding, melting anything in its path.

He'd hated that anger. It reminded him of his parents, of his mother's shrill rage and his father's outraged roaring. Of standing in that airport as the two of them had yanked him back and forth, fighting over him as if he was a bone between two dogs. Of the feverish brightness in his mother's bright eyes as she'd poured him that orange juice, and the satisfaction in his father's expression as he'd told Cesare that he was forbidding Bianca to see him.

No one could understand what had happened in their marriage to make the two of them hate each other like that. Cesare had read all about it in the media, the articles and the think pieces, the theories on why, but he knew, because he felt it himself.

The why was in the ferocity of his anger, an anger that had come from love.

Love was the issue. Love was the problem.

He'd loved his parents, yet they'd continually made him feel as if he was failing one or the other of them, and so that love had turned to rage. He hated them now and that hate was the same hate they'd turned on each other, which was why he had to be careful.

Anger could turn into toxicity so quickly, and he himself might have been consumed back when he was younger, if he hadn't funnelled it into determination. A determination to not let his parents ruin his life. To not be scarred by it or harmed by it. To come out of it unmarked and strong and successful.

So that's what he'd done. Yet his anger was still with him, still bubbling away under the surface. He'd thought he'd managed to get rid of it, but clearly he hadn't, which meant he'd made a mistake somewhere along the line.

He'd let himself care; that was the issue. He'd let himself care about Lark, about what she thought of him, and now he was angry that he cared. So he'd thrown his own selfishness back in her face so she knew what kind of man he was. Yet she hadn't flinched from him. She'd only looked at him levelly and told him not to demonise himself, that he wasn't selfish and why would he think he was?

He didn't like that and he didn't like the way she was staring at him now, with an expression of sympathy and understanding. Looking at him as if he was still that hurt little boy all those years ago.

'Don't look at me like that,' he said abruptly. 'I don't need your pity. It was years ago. I am done with it now and I am done with them.'

'It's not pity.' Her voice was quiet. 'I'm sad and horrified for you, Cesare, and I'm sorry you had that happen to you. No child should be treated that way. To be fought over like a…a possession. And then to make you feel as if you were to blame—'

'I don't feel that way,' he interrupted harshly. 'Not any more.'

She didn't even blink. 'Don't you? You're certainly still angry with them.'

'Perhaps,' he forced out, not wanting to admit it, yet not being able to deny it either. 'But having you and Maya here will be a new beginning. A way to leave this particular piece of the past behind.'

Lark nodded slowly, studying him for a long moment, making discomfort twist inside him. He didn't like the way she looked at him, as if she could see right through him, through every lie he'd told himself since his parents' death, even the lie that he was done with both it and them.

Then she said, 'You have every right to be angry with them, Cesare. They were terrible parents and they should have done better.'

It was such a simple statement and trite in its way. Yet he felt something twist inside him, though he wasn't sure what it was. He didn't want to examine it, though. Neither did he want a conversation about his own motivations and thoughts with Lark.

'Yes,' he agreed, keeping his voice very neutral. 'They should. But now you know my history and Maya's.' He took a step towards her, taking his hands from his pockets. 'Come upstairs with me. I want you naked.'

She didn't move, her gaze level. Today she wore a plain blue linen dress that caught the blue hints in her green eyes and her golden hair was loose and curling over her shoulders. It wasn't a white wedding dress, but she didn't need a white dress to look feminine and delicate, like a princess. A princess he wanted to ravish completely.

His wife now.

If you'd really wanted to create a different legacy you should have had a different beginning. You should have married her properly. Given her a beautiful dress and a wonderful ceremony, then taken her on a honeymoon that she'd remember for ever.

Perhaps he should, but it was too late now. It was done. He'd been impatient to get his ring on her finger and now she was his wife.

The primal, possessive part of him, the part that he never let out from its cage, growled like a beast. He wanted her in his bed and now, and what he wanted he got.

He'd told her he was selfish and what he wanted was all that mattered.

He stalked towards her, closing the distance, loving the way she gave a little gasp as he reached out and gripped her by the hips, pulling her hard up against him. She was all soft and warm against the hard length of his sex, and he was starting to think that maybe he'd just have her here, on the sofa. Or perhaps he'd bend her over it. Either way would suit him nicely.

Lark lifted her hands and put them on his chest, not pushing him, but certainly holding him at bay.

'Wait,' she said breathlessly. 'I need us to discuss a few things first.'

'Things?' He slid his hands over her rear, fitting the soft heat between her thighs over his aching groin, impatience gripping him. 'What things?'

Lark's hands remained firm on his chest. Her face was

delightfully flushed, but the expression in her eyes was all determination. 'I told you, Cesare. Our marriage.'

'You wanted my history so I gave it.' He flexed his hips against her, watching with satisfaction as her gaze darkened, arousal glowing hot beneath her determination. 'What else do you need?'

She took a sharp breath. 'It's not just that, and it's not just being in your bed and living together. It's about how we treat each other. That will have an effect on Maya—you can't deny that. We're both living examples of it after all.'

She's right. She has thought about this. Have you?

No, if he was honest with himself, he hadn't. All he'd thought about was making her and Maya his and then having Lark in his bed. That was the extent of it. And he was finding it difficult to think about it now, because her warmth and vanilla scent was driving him crazy.

Still, she had a point, they did need to talk about it. 'We can discuss later, surely?' he asked, his voice now slightly roughed with desire.

'I don't want us to start this marriage off in a way that might end badly for all of us.' There was doubt in her eyes beneath the determination and the arousal, and that doubt caught at him. He didn't like it. He didn't want her doubting this new life. He wanted her feeling safe and secure and happy.

So he forced his desire aside for a moment and met her gaze. 'I don't either,' he said, letting her see the conviction in his eyes. 'So know that I will always treat you with the utmost respect. Any issues or disagreements we have, we discuss privately and do everything we can to find a compromise if we can't agree. Aside from that, you and I will share a bed every night, but during the day we can go our own ways. We will come together as a family when it's required for Maya, and we will never, ever argue about her in front of her.'

Lark stared up at him silently for a long moment, searching his face. Then the doubt in her eyes began to fade. 'We both want what's best for her, don't we?'

'Yes,' he agreed and meant it. 'She comes first. Always.'

Lark's hands relaxed, desire glowing bright in her eyes. Then her fingers curled in the material of his shirt and she tugged him close. 'Good,' she murmured. 'I like the sound of that.'

Then she went up on her toes and pressed her mouth to his.

CHAPTER NINE

LARK FOUND THE next few weeks unexpectedly happy.

For all that Cesare had told her that they'd go their separate ways during the day, he ended up staying at the palazzo quite a lot. He told her he was 'working from home' but seemed to spend a good deal of his time with Maya. Helping her 'settle in', apparently.

Not that she was complaining.

Not when every night she was naked in his bed, in his arms.

There was so much pleasure to be had from him, and yet another reason why she didn't understand why he thought he was selfish, not when he was the opposite in bed.

He was inventive when it came to wringing orgasms from her, encouraging her to tell him what she wanted and how, then welcoming her passion whenever she gave it. He never refused her anything and seemed to get as much enjoyment from her pleasure as he did from his own.

There was nothing selfish about that, nothing at all.

Some mornings she'd come down to breakfast in the palazzo to find him lying on the ground with his daughter, letting her climb all over him and pull on his expensive silk tie with her dirty hands, or playing trucks, which really just consisted of banging them on the ground. Once, she'd come down to find Maya asleep in the crook of his arm and him singing softly to her in Italian.

That in particular had caught at her heart, her daughter's red-gold curls nestled against the dark wool of his suit, golden eyelashes fanned over her rosy cheeks. He'd been looking down at her as he sang and the expression on his face had stolen her breath. She'd had to look away, feeling as if she'd invaded his privacy somehow.

He'd told her the day they'd got married that it wasn't Maya who was important to him, but his legacy, and maybe he believed that. But it wasn't true and Lark knew it. Not when he'd also said, not five minutes later that Maya came first, always.

Whether he knew it or not, he loved his daughter. It was written all over his face.

He didn't just spend time with Maya, though. He was very insistent that they do things together 'as a family'. Again, not something she'd object to, since she enjoyed those things as much as she suspected he did.

Sometimes it was as simple as having dinner outside on one of the terraces, with Maya in a highchair and Cesare insisting on feeding her himself as he listened to Lark tell him about Maya's day. Afterwards, they'd lie on a blanket on the lawn, in the warm summer evening scented with the lavender that grew in the garden beds nearby, idly chatting about nothing as Maya played with her growing collection of trucks.

Sometimes it was more of an outing, such as the time Cesare took them to spend a few days in Venice in a luxurious palace beside the canals. They'd had gondola rides and Maya had squealed with delight at the pigeons in the Piazza San Marco.

He took them to other places around Italy too, Tuscany and the Cinque Terre, to Florence and Naples, and Milan. He said he wanted to show Maya the country since she was part Italian, but Lark had a sneaking suspicion that he wasn't quite telling the truth about that. Because Maya was very little and probably wouldn't remember or appreciate the beautiful scenery, but Lark did. Lark did very much.

Then in Rome, after a day spent wandering the streets with Maya in a buggy and all three of them eating gelato, Cesare organised a private tour of the Colosseum, and even though Lark had told him she'd already seen it, he insisted she go. Because Maya hadn't seen it, he told her, and neither had she, not without all the crowds.

Privately Lark doubted Maya needed to see the Colosseum just yet, but she didn't really mind. Yet as they stood there in the ruins of a once mighty empire, Cesare bent and picked Maya up, putting her up on his shoulders, and as her squeals of delight rang off the ancient stones, Lark remembered standing in this same place nearly two years earlier. And she'd watched a family standing together like this, a child on their father's shoulders, the mother standing by. And she'd been hit by such a feeling of such isolation and loneliness, or wishing she'd had a family just like that one.

Now she had, yet it wasn't the same. Not quite.

She had a daughter and a husband, but their marriage was lacking one thing. They were only married for Maya's sake not their own, and while she and Cesare loved Maya, they didn't love each other.

They respected each other—he'd kept his promise to her that he'd treat her with nothing but respect—but love wasn't a part of that.

Why do you need love? You didn't want it, remember?

She hadn't, no. But now the lack of it made her worry for the future of their little family. Cesare had promised that Maya always came first and she agreed, but would that be enough to hold them together?

If she'd learned anything from her unsettled childhood it was that a broken relationship between a child's parents could hurt their child, and Cesare too had been a prime example of that.

She didn't want that kind of tragedy for her daughter. Not that she thought she and Cesare would suddenly turn on each other like their respective parents' had, nevertheless… He'd promised he'd be faithful, but what if he got tired of sleeping with her? What if he wanted someone else? What would happen and what would she do?

The very thought of it sent a hot, bright bolt of unexpected jealousy straight through her, and because Cesare had chosen that moment to glance at her, she'd had to turn away quickly in order to hide it.

How ridiculous to be jealous. He'd been very clear that love was something he didn't want, and that they'd be sleeping together only as long as this desire lasted and then they'd be done.

She'd agreed to it. She'd let him put that ring on her finger. She'd known exactly what a marriage to him had meant. Being jealous hadn't never been part of this scenario.

You never thought you'd feel something for him, though.

Lark's stomach dropped away.

The tour guide's voice rose and fell, but she'd stopped listening.

She *did* feel something for him, it was nestled there close to her heart, and what it was, she didn't know and didn't want to. But whatever it was, it made the thought of him finding some other woman to hold at night… difficult.

A selfish man wouldn't have noticed her sudden quiet. A selfish man wouldn't have paid any attention to her at all. Yet after the tour was over and as they got in the car to return to the palazzo, Cesare glanced at her. 'You're very quiet, little bird. Is anything wrong?'

She couldn't tell him about that jealousy, about that feeling in her heart, not when she didn't have the words for it herself, so instead she pasted on her sunniest, most cheerful smile. 'No, of course not. Why would there be? I've had the loveliest day.'

He looked as if he was going to say something more, but right then Maya dropped her soft rabbit on the floor of the car and started shouting with annoyance, which distracted Cesare nicely.

She should have known better than to think he'd forgotten, though.

When they'd got home and a very tired Maya had been settled in bed, Cesare slid an arm around her waist and pulled her in close in the hallway outside Maya's door.

'Now that I finally have you alone,' he murmured. 'You can tell me what's wrong.'

Lark swallowed, the familiar warmth of his body against hers working its magic.

Damn him. She couldn't tell him and it certainly

wasn't worth upsetting the balance they'd found in their marriage to even try articulating her strange doubts.

And it would upset it. She had no idea what he'd think about her feelings for him, but he certainly wouldn't like it.

'Nothing.' She took a breath and then forced herself to look up at him, giving him the same bright smile that she always gave her mother. 'Honestly. I was just a bit tired earlier.'

His gaze narrowed into glowing blue sapphire splinters. 'You can smile at me like that till kingdom come, little bird, and I still won't believe you.'

Annoyance gripped her. That smile had always worked for her mother. Why wouldn't it work for him?

'There's nothing—'

'Lark.' His hands tightened on her hips. 'You went very quiet at the Colosseum today and wouldn't look me in the eye after the tour. Why? Something's bothering you and I want to know what.'

She couldn't help herself, she had to glance away. He'd see straight through her, because he always seemed to. He'd see her jealousy and the feeling that was growing inside her, the fear that she didn't want to examine or even articulate.

That she was falling for him.

Instead she stared at the buttons of his casual black shirt and put her hands on his chest, feeling the steady beat of his heart, trying to think of something to say that wasn't the truth and coming up with nothing. 'It doesn't matter, Cesare,' she said at last. 'Leave it.'

But then her chin was being gripped in long fingers as he forced her gaze up to meet his. 'Why do you do that?' he demanded abruptly. 'Why do you smile and pretend nothing's wrong?'

Her annoyance deepened. 'I'm not pretending.'

'Yes, you are. I can see it in your eyes and your smile is fake as hell.'

The annoyance became anger and for a minute it was all she could do not to snap and rip herself from his arms. And she didn't want to snap. She didn't want to ruin what had been a perfectly nice day with a foul temper.

'Little bird,' Cesare said, quieter this time, the look in his eyes softening unexpectedly. 'You don't have to pretend with me, you know that, don't you?'

She wasn't sure why her anger faltered right then. Why it simply flickered and went out like a candle flame. Perhaps it was because of his gentle reminder when she'd been expecting him to argue, or the concern in his eyes when she'd been expecting irritation.

And that was the thing, wasn't it? She'd never pretended with him. She'd never been able to, not even right from the very beginning.

So she let herself relax against him, lean into his warmth and his strength. 'I know,' she said. 'It's just… Mum was so fragile emotionally and getting angry or being in a bad mood always made her worse. Even just being sad was an issue. And I…didn't want to make things harder for her than they already were. So… I made sure I was always in a good mood, that I was always smiling, because it was easier for both of us if I was.'

Cesare's thumb stroked over her chin in a gentle movement. 'Well, I'm not your mother, Lark Donati. I'm your husband and I'm not afraid of your temper, and you know that. We wouldn't be standing right here if I was.'

Lark felt something inside her ease, a tightness that she hadn't realised was there. 'That's true,' she admitted. 'You never have been.'

He was frowning, though. 'I don't like that she made you feel responsible for her moods.'

'She wasn't well,' Lark said. 'I didn't want to add to it. And sometimes—' She broke off all of a sudden, not wanting to say the doubt out loud, because part of her didn't want her to acknowledge it even to herself.

'Sometimes?' Cesare let go of her hips, only to thread his fingers through her hair, holding her gently as he looked down into her eyes. 'What about sometimes?'

She sighed. 'Sometimes I used to wonder if she wouldn't have been happier if I hadn't been born at all. Then she wouldn't have had to go on the run and maybe she wouldn't have—'

'She might,' Cesare interrupted gently. 'But also, she might not have. Also, as a parent, I know that even though Maya completely upended my life and yours, I'd much rather she was born than not.'

Lark let out a breath and the words she'd been keeping inside for far too long came spilling out along with it. 'There was nothing I could do to fix her,' she said huskily. 'I tried to be happy, tried to keep smiling. Tried to stay optimistic. But nothing worked. Or it would work for a bit, but then she'd spiral again. Sometimes, she'd stay in her room with the door locked for days and days.' Her throat tightened, the old fear flooding back. 'And I used to be so afraid that one day she wouldn't come out.'

Cesare's blue gaze somehow became no less fierce, no less sharp, and yet there was something protective in it that wrapped around her heart and pulled tight. 'I know your mother was in a difficult situation and that she was afraid. And that she might have been sick, as well, but why did she not get help?'

'It was difficult, because she didn't want anyone to know our names in case my father found us.'

'So what provision did she make for you?' His fingers tightened in her hair. 'What if one day she actually hadn't come out of that room? What would have happened to you then?'

Unexpectedly, Lark felt her tears fill her eyes. She'd been so afraid back then, and sometimes she wondered if perhaps her mother had infected her with her own fear and paranoia, that it was a vicious circle, each of them feeding off the other's fear.

'I don't know,' she said huskily. 'She didn't have any friends and wouldn't allow me to have any either. She thought the less people who knew about us the better.'

Cesare's mouth hardened and she saw the blue glow of anger in his eyes. But not at her she knew.

'You can't get angry at her,' she said, feeling protective. 'She did the best she could.'

'No, she didn't.' His voice was flat. 'The best she could would have been not to make you responsible for her wellbeing. That was her job, not yours.'

It was her most secret doubt, the anger that she kept locked tight away inside her. Anger at Grace for doing exactly that, for ensuring her childhood was one town after another, a cheap flat, a grotty motel room, a stranger's basement…

No friends. No steady school. Only fear and the sense that she was always walking on eggshells around her mother, never sure what would send her into another depressive incident. The knowledge that she was the one who had to look after Grace, not the other way around.

Lark felt hot tears fill her eyes, though she wasn't sure why. Maybe just the fact that he'd said it aloud and it was such a relief to have someone else acknowledge it. 'I was…angry at her,' she said. 'I know it wasn't her fault and that she wanted to protect me, and I loved her. But I'm angry with her all the same.'

'You can love someone and be angry with them at the same time,' he said. 'And I know it doesn't change things, but you should have had better, Lark.'

He believed it, she could see. There was a fierceness to his stare that for some reason felt like cold water on a burn, easing her. Soothing her.

'Thanks,' she said huskily. 'That helps. And you know what? I don't even feel angry any more.'

'Good.' The fierceness in his stare somehow intensified. 'Then you won't mind telling me what was bothering you earlier, will you?'

Cesare saw reluctance flicker through Lark's wide sea-green eyes. She didn't want to tell him, that was clear, though he couldn't imagine why, not when over the course of the past few weeks they'd grown closer.

Having her here at the palazzo, in his bed at night and waking up to her in the morning, then sharing coffee on the terrace as Maya played at their feet…it had been so unexpectedly fulfilling. And while he still saw flashes of her delightful temper, she'd started to relax with him, the truth of her becoming apparent, so warm and open and genuine. Intelligent, funny and honest too.

She was a delight. The way she'd been that night two years ago.

Their daughter too was a delight.

He also hadn't realised how completely fascinating having a child was. How a deep part of him kept getting drawn to this little girl with the big blue eyes the same colour as his own. Maya, too, had a temper that he admired and she was also very stubborn, which he also admired. She was very loud sometimes and he admired that less, but he respected her commitment to it.

She'd started smiling for him now and lifting her arms to him whenever she saw him, and he was sure she'd babbled *Papa* at him on more than one occasion.

He had no words to describe the strength of feeling inside him on those occasions.

The only thing he knew was that going places with his little family or even just staying at home with them had made him for the first time in his life…happy.

This was what he'd wanted to give his child that he'd never had himself. This happiness. He'd once thought that all families were like his, that most parents screamed and hated each other like his did, but it wasn't until after they'd gone that he'd understood that no, most families weren't like that.

Perhaps it had been then that all the anger he'd suppressed while he'd been a child trying to make two irrational people happy had started spilling out like poison. Anger at them and what they'd put him through, the childhood he'd been denied. Happiness. Security. Love.

All his parents had given him was their own rage, which they'd nurtured with their dysfunctional relationship and so now he was cursed with it too. There was no escape for him. There was always the doubt that if he gave in to it, he'd turn into them, violent and irrational and toxic.

But he'd been good these past few weeks. The simmering rage that had burned just beneath the surface of his skin had receded back down to where he'd buried it deep inside, and hopefully now it was gone for good. It hadn't touched Maya or Lark, and he was glad.

He'd been feeling very glad at the Colosseum today, too, enjoying the feeling of Maya's warm little body on his shoulders and hearing her laugh. He'd turned to glance at Lark to see if she was enjoying herself as much as he was, only to catch a glimpse of some troubled expression on her eyes, something painful. Then she'd looked away, avoiding his gaze.

A strange feeling had stolen through him then, an urge to find out what it was that was hurting her and take it away, soothe her. It was unfamiliar this feeling, yet he hadn't questioned it after they'd got into the car. He'd asked her straight out what was wrong, but she'd only smiled, told him it was nothing and turned away.

Maya losing her toy had distracted him, yet he hadn't forgotten. The smile Lark had given him had been fake. And he knew the difference. He'd been seeing Lark's genuine smiles for the past few weeks, after all. When she held Maya in her arms and looked down at her. When he kept the light on at night, so he could watch her face as he made love to her, and after he'd given her as much pleasure as they both could handle, and after they'd both recovered, she'd smile slowly, like the sun coming up, lighting her face, lighting her green eyes.

That was a real smile. But the one she'd given him in the car was not.

Perhaps he should have let it go, but he couldn't. The knowledge that something was bothering her nagged at him like a shard of glass caught in a place he couldn't reach, and he knew that he couldn't ignore it. He had to find out what was wrong.

Her happiness was vital to his new legacy plan, which meant he had to fix it.

He'd got sidetracked by talk of her mother and he could see now why she'd been pretending today. It had made him inexplicably angry the way she'd been treated as a child, the burden of responsibility that had been put on her shoulders by her mother, and he'd found himself wishing he could change it. Go back in time and tell Grace Edwards to get out of her head and look at what she was doing to her daughter. An irrational wish. Nevertheless he wished it. But all he could do was tell Lark that she shouldn't have had to deal with that, that it had been wrong of her mother, and hope Lark believed him. Also, that he wasn't her mother and she didn't need to do that with him.

Lark's lashes lowered, veiling her gaze as she toyed with one of the buttons on his shirt. 'It's nothing,' she said slowly. 'Only…that night we met two years ago, I'd also just been to the Colosseum and I saw a family there. Parents and a child, and they were having so much fun. I remember wishing I could have had that as a kid.' She let out a long breath and looked up at him. 'Then we were there today and I realised I did have it. With you and Maya.'

He frowned, dropping his hands to her hips and then

lower, sliding over the curve of her rear to bring her closer, where he preferred her. 'You didn't look happy, though,' he said. 'You looked as if someone had stabbed you.'

She stared up at him for a long moment. Then abruptly she pushed herself away and out of his arms. His first instinct was to grab her and pull her back, but he crushed the urge. If she wanted space then he had to let her have it. Her needs were important to his plan and he couldn't let himself forget it.

'What's going to happen, Cesare?' she asked. 'When you find someone you want more than me? When you get tired of me? What will we do?'

His frown deepened. He didn't understand why she was asking him this. 'What has that got to do with you realising you have a family?'

'That family I saw, they loved each other.' Lark's voice was flat. 'All of them loved each other.'

'So?' He still didn't quite see what she was getting at.

'Our marriage isn't a real marriage,' she said. 'We're only together for Maya's sake. So what happens if it breaks down between us? What happens if you decide you want someone else?'

'Our marriage is very real,' he insisted, slightly irritated because they'd already had this discussion right before she agreed to marry him. 'You've taken my name. You wear my ring. You sleep in my bed. We live together. How is that not real?'

'Because we don't…care about other, do we?' There was an odd pain glittering in her eyes that he didn't quite understand. 'And it's the children that suffer when two people don't care about each other, Cesare. You know that and so do I.'

A flicker of shock went through him, because he hadn't been expecting this. It felt as if she'd taken a hammer to the most perfect mirror and now there was a crack running straight through it.

How could she think he didn't care about her? When he'd done nothing but make sure she was happy for the past three weeks?

'That's not true,' he said, itching to grab her and drag her back into his arms and show her just how wrong she was. 'I do care about you. Haven't I been proving it to you since we got married? Haven't you been happy these past few weeks?'

She let out a breath, the expression on her face difficult to read. 'Yes,' she said, almost reluctantly. 'I have. I just…want Maya to know what a good relationship looks like. What respect means. I want her to know what a good man looks like.'

That hit him hard, in a place where he knew he was vulnerable. Because he wanted that for Maya too, but he wasn't a good man. He never had been.

You'll just have to try harder then, won't you?

Yes. He would.

'I agree,' he said. 'And she will know, Lark. I promise on her life that she will know.'

Lark said nothing, her gaze was unreadable and he didn't like it.

'What more do you want?' He was impatient now to get whatever this was out of the way so they could get on with being happy. 'Tell me and I'll give it to you.'

She remained silent a moment more, then said, 'I don't

want you to sleep with anyone else while Maya is still a child. You'll be faithful to me and I'll be faithful to you.'

He hadn't even thought about another woman since being with Lark and couldn't imagine being with one either. So he answered without hesitation. 'I don't want another woman, Lark. I want you.'

'Promise me, Cesare.'

He couldn't ignore his instinct any longer. Reaching out, he pulled her back into his arms, settling her where she belonged, against him. 'I am not going to get tired of you,' he said. 'In fact, I can't see myself wanting anyone else for a long, long time. So yes, while Maya is growing up, the only woman in my bed will be you. I promise.'

Lark's gaze was searching as she looked up into his face, so he let her see the truth, the force of his conviction to his promise.

Is this really just for the sake of your legacy now? Or is this for her?

But he didn't understand that thought, because the two were the same, so he ignored it.

'You mean that?' Lark asked, the tension slowly bleeding out of her.

He raised a brow. 'Do you want me to write out another agreement?'

'God no.' She flushed. 'I think I've had my fill of legal documents from you.'

He laughed, pulling her closer as satisfaction stretched out inside him. 'Does that mean you trust me, little bird? Trust me to keep my promise?'

'Yes,' she said on a long breath. 'I do.'

'Good. Now let's seal the deal.'

And he bent his head and covered her mouth with his own.

CHAPTER TEN

LARK STOOD IN the doorway to the terrace, watching her husband as he sat at the big stone outside table with Maya in his lap. She'd just turned two and Cesare had wanted to do something special to mark the occasion, so they'd had a small afternoon party with a few of her friends from the little play group she attended with Emily.

All their guests had gone now except one: Aristophanes Katsaros, who owned one of the biggest finance companies on the planet and was apparently Cesare's closest friend.

Lark had been slightly startled that Cesare even had a close friend, let alone that he'd invited him to Maya's birthday. Especially since Aristophanes had seemed absolutely mystified by the little girl.

He and Cesare were talking now in fast and fluid Italian, and as Lark watched, Maya slid off her father's lap and toddled over to where Aristophanes was sitting. She tugged on his trouser leg and lifted her arms to him, apparently unafraid of this stern stranger. Cesare laughed as his friend, with obvious reluctance, lifted the child up and gazed at her in apparent bewilderment.

Amusement stole through Lark. Aristophanes was an inch or so taller than Cesare, which put him at nearly six-five, with black hair and the kind of steel grey eyes that looked like storm clouds. He was definitely a…presence. He tended towards unsmiling silence, his grey gaze watchful, but there was something very compelling about him.

Clearly Maya thought so too, because she babbled happily at him, while he stared back in stunned silence.

The afternoon had been a wonderful one, with the little ones running around on the lawn with lots of games and sweet treats. Maya had loved it. She'd especially loved being carried around by her father all day as he showed her off to all the guests like the little princess she was. Lark had felt her heart clench tight in her chest every time.

These past nine months had been so wonderful. Since the night he'd promised her that he wouldn't be with anyone else, easing her doubts, she'd felt so much more secure. Safe, almost, and she hadn't been able to say that for a very long time.

Cesare had been a caring, attentive husband, not only keeping her happy at night, but also helping her enrol in university, and supporting her as she worked her way towards an art history degree. She wasn't sure what she was going to do with it yet, but after her training with Mr Ravenswood, she'd become interested in antiquities and the preservation of them. She was now thinking she might like to do some museum studies, but she wasn't quite sure yet.

There was no pressure, though. She was creating a life for herself and a home here in Italy with Cesare and she loved it.

She leaned her head against the doorframe, watching

him as he finally took pity on Aristophanes and took Maya from him, tossing her into the air a couple of times and making her squeal with excitement. The look on his face was so full of joy it made her chest hurt.

It had been hurting like that for the last few months, whenever she saw him with their daughter. He'd had such a terrible upbringing, with parents who hadn't cared about him, with one even trying to kill him, yet he hadn't let that stop him from being the best father to his child. He was so wonderful with her, never letting his own terrible history touch her.

She didn't understand why he'd ever thought of himself as selfish. She didn't understand anything when it came to him.

You do. You understand too much.

Her mouth dried, her eyes prickling. Perhaps she did understand. Perhaps she'd been lying to herself all this time, telling herself that she didn't know what the feeling that gripped her whenever she looked at him with their daughter, whenever he took her in his arms, was.

The feeling that had wound itself around her heart and made itself part of her.

He'd made good on every single promise he'd given her and since that night where they'd talked outside Maya's room, he'd never given her a single moment's doubt either.

He made her so happy.

He was beautiful inside and out.

Lark's vision swam and her throat tightened as she felt that feeling grow bigger, taking up every part of her, making it hard to breathe.

It was love. She knew it with every cell of her being.

Somehow, at some point in the past few months, she'd committed a cardinal sin and fallen in love with her husband.

She turned away, her heart beating far too hard, furiously blinking away her tears.

Love had never been what she wanted—had never been what either of them wanted—and yet it had happened all the same.

He accepted all the passionate feelings that lived inside her that she'd had to keep under control for her mother's sake, and had never turned away from them, not once. He even liked her anger as he'd told her on more than one occasion.

And all through these difficult months of starting a new life in a new country, he'd been there supporting her. Caring for her and her daughter, damn him.

Now she understood why she'd trusted him the night she had no memory of. Why she'd told him everything, why she'd given herself to him. Perhaps she'd even fallen in love with him that night and now, here she was doing it all over again.

Now, it was all so clear.

He'd made himself so much a part of her life, she couldn't imagine being without him.

He'd told her that all of this would be his new legacy, a new start for the Donati family, and that was what was important to him. Not Maya and not her. He kept insisting that he was selfish, that he wasn't a good man, and yet everything he did proved the opposite.

She wanted to show him that. Show him what an incredible man he was and what a fantastic father he'd been, and make him believe it.

She wanted to make him as happy as he'd made her.

She wanted to love him. Yet that was the one thing he didn't want.

So? What difference does it make? You have a life with him that's already perfect, so why not keep things as they are?

Lark pushed herself away from the doorframe and stepped into the cool of the salon, trying to get a breath.

She desperately wanted to keep things as they were, but there had been rare occasions where he'd shut himself away in his study or left on a business trip and not asked her to join him. Moments where there were shadows in his blue eyes and a tension in his powerful shoulders. And it was in those moments that she wanted to ask him what was wrong, to help him the way he'd helped her. Soothe him. Love him. But whenever she asked about it, he'd brush it aside, change the subject or simply kiss her and distract her with pleasure.

He wouldn't let her in and he never would. Because he'd told her right at the start of this marriage, and nothing had changed, not for him.

Yet everything had changed for her. Everything.

Your love wasn't enough to make your mother happy. Why would it be enough for him?

Tears slid down her cheeks.

It would never be enough. His past was too dark, his wounds too deep. Some hurts couldn't be healed with a smile and a good mood, and she knew that all too well.

She didn't know what to do. Leaving him wasn't an option. Cesare loved his daughter so much, and Maya loved him too, she saw it every day in her daughter's eyes. Lark would never tear them apart by taking Maya from him, never.

Leaving without Maya also wasn't an option. She couldn't bear to leave her child. Her falling in love wasn't Maya's fault after all.

But she had to do something, protect herself somehow. Loving someone who didn't want it was a terrible thing and she didn't want the relationship she had with Cesare to break down because of her own hurt feelings.

Which left her with only one option. She had to tell Cesare that she couldn't sleep with him any more, that she couldn't be his wife, not in that way. Friendship was all she could do, and at the moment she wasn't even sure she could do that.

It would hurt him. He'd probably be furious, but there wasn't any other way. Not if she wanted to keep this little life she'd made for herself and Maya.

'Little bird?'

Cesare's deep voice, full of warmth and tenderness, came from behind her and she caught her breath, wiping frantically at her eyes.

Then she turned, forcing a smile on her face. 'What is it?'

He stood in the doorway, casual today in a black T-shirt and worn faded jeans, and she loved him as much in casual clothes as she did when he was in a suit, perhaps even more so.

He looked relaxed, his beautiful mouth curving in a smile he kept just for her. He was so beautiful. Everything about him, from the exquisite planes and angles of his perfect face to his eyes, a deeper blue than even a summer sky.

But even more than his physical beauty, she knew the beauty of his soul. He thought he kept it hidden from her, but she saw it all the same. She saw it in his eyes every time he looked at Maya, even now with wonder, as if he couldn't believe she existed.

He was a good man. He didn't believe it, she knew, but he was.

'I've invited Aristophanes to stay for dinner,' he said. 'You don't mind?'

'No,' she said, her voice husky. 'Of course I don't mind. He's most welcome to stay.'

A faint frown crossed his brow. 'Are you all right?'

No, she wasn't all right. She was desperately in love with him and she didn't know what to do. Or rather, she did know what to do, she just didn't want to do it.

Sooner rather than later. You'll only make it worse for yourself by waiting.

She would, but she couldn't do it now, not with his friend here.

But even later, after Maya was in bed and Aristophanes had left, she could hardly bring herself to say the words she needed to say. And what made it worse was after they'd both sorted through Maya's birthday cards, and organised all the new toys she'd got for her birthday, Cesare pulled Lark close in the hallway and ran his hands over her, making it clear what he wanted.

There was no perfect time to tell him of her decision, but…she could have one last time with him, couldn't she? She could never resist him and one last night to touch him, kiss his beautiful mouth, have him inside her wasn't so much to ask, was it? He'd been talking about having another child and she couldn't think of anything she wanted more than to have another of his babies.

Except how could she bring another child into the world whose parents' relationship was so fraught?

Especially when you already have one who might be hurt by your decision.

No, and there were no good solutions either. Everywhere she turned someone was going to be hurt, no matter how hard she tried to limit the damage.

'I want you,' Cesare murmured in her ear, as he kissed his way down her neck, his hands stroking down her sides. 'Let me take you to bed, little bird.'

And abruptly Lark was tired of thinking about it, tired of the pain shredding her heart. She wanted him, wanted this, and if it was the last time, so be it. She'd take it.

'Yes,' she whispered and let herself relax against his chest as he picked her up and took her upstairs to their bedroom.

As he set her down next to the bed, his hands already at the zip of her dress, she abruptly pulled away. Her heart was beating far too fast and she was desperate for him in a way she hadn't felt before, but she wanted to do this her way.

'No,' she said huskily, turning to face him. 'Let me undress you first. I want to touch you.'

He smiled, the beauty of it making her ache. 'Be my guest.'

He never denied her anything when it came to sex, yet part of her wished he'd deny her now, because this was only going to make it harder for her.

Still, she stepped up close to him, taking the hem of his T-shirt in her hands and drawing it up slowly, exposing his flat, chiselled stomach and smooth olive skin. Then she lifted it higher and he raised his arms, helping her get the fabric off the rest of the way.

Dropping the T-shirt on the floor, she then let her hands wander over his bare chest, feeling the hard muscle beneath his warm satiny skin and the crisp prickle of hair.

He felt so amazing. He always did.

Leaning forward she kissed her way along his pecs, her fingers trailing down to his narrow hips, then toying with the buttons of his jeans. He made a delicious sound of male satisfaction, one of his large warm hands cradling the back of her head as she continued to kiss her way down his rock-hard torso, undoing his jeans then sliding her hands inside.

He growled, his fingers clenching tight in her hair as she took the long, thick, hard length of him in her hand, stroking him, teasing him.

She loved him. She loved his body and the sounds he made. The way he touched her when he was aroused. And he should know that he was loved, know that he was cared for. No one had ever cared for him; no one had loved him. She couldn't bear it.

She didn't want to ruin this moment by telling him, but she would show him. She would worship him the way he deserved to be worshipped.

Kneeling at his feet, she slid his jeans down over his hips, taking his underwear with them, and he stepped out of the fabric, finally, gloriously naked.

Lark ran her hands up his powerful thighs to the hard length of his sex. He was beautiful there too and he should know it. She leaned forward and took him in her mouth, tasting his delicious flavour, all salt and musk and heat.

He made another deep growling sound, his fingers a fist in her hair as she drew him in deep. 'My beautiful wife.' His voice was low and rough. 'You make me so hungry.'

He made her hungry too. He made her want more. He made her want everything. But she couldn't ask that of him, not when he'd been so clear what love meant to him.

It wasn't his fault she wanted something more.

Eventually he got impatient and pulled her up from where she knelt, tossing her on the bed and following her down, pinning her beneath him. 'Now,' he murmured. 'Where were we?' Then he pulled her clothing off and she helped, desperate to have nothing between them but skin.

So when he reached for a condom in the bedside table drawer, she stopped him. 'No,' she said when he looked down at her in surprise. 'You wanted another child. Let's try for one.' She could give him this gift, couldn't she?

But what about your decision?

Maybe she didn't have to leave him now. Maybe she'd wait to see if she was pregnant and then make a decision. She just hadn't realised how much it would hurt.

Cesare smiled at her and it was as if the sun had come up on a bitter winter landscape, the promise of summer and warmth and life.

It made her want to cry, but instead she reached up and pulled his mouth down on hers, kissing him desperately, gasping in pleasure as he slid inside her.

He felt so right. So perfect. She wanted to keep him there for ever.

She wound her legs around his waist, holding him where he was, and when he put his hands on either side of her head and looked down into her eyes, she stared back. She couldn't help herself.

He began to move, deep and slow, and she could see the pleasure glow bright in his gaze, and the hunger too.

His eyes were so blue.

She loved him so much.

She wanted to tell him so, but she couldn't do that now. He'd stop and she didn't want him to stop. Instead, she raised her hand and touched his beautiful face the way she had on the plane that day, so long ago now. Tracing his features as he moved inside her, the pleasure growing deeper and deeper.

'Lark,' he said softly, turning to brush his mouth over her fingertips. 'My little bird.'

Yes, she was his. She'd be his for ever; she knew it deep in her soul.

The orgasm hit her without warning, hard and fast and when it did, she had to bury her face in his neck to stop the tears that came along with it.

Cesare felt the orgasm hit, pleasure pouring through him, and he couldn't move for long moments. Not that he wanted to. He was quite happy with Lark lying beneath him, all soft and hot, her legs wrapped around his waist, her face turned against his neck.

Every part of him was relaxed and heavy with physical satiation, pleasure echoing through him, yet something was bothering him and he couldn't figure out what.

Then he realised that Lark was weeping.

Shock cut through the pleasure like a knife, and he

moved off her, lying on his side and looking down at her. Tears were rolling down her cheeks. She turned away, flinging an arm across her eyes as if she was trying to hide from him.

His chest tightened and he grabbed her arm, pulling it away so he could see her face. It was flushed and wet with tears.

'Lark?' he demanded, rougher than he'd intended. 'Did I hurt you?' Fear gripped him. Had he done something terrible? He must have to make her weep like this. 'Lark,' he said again, trying to pull her close. But she wriggled out of his grip, turning away.

He stared at her, bewildered by her sudden change in mood. She'd been so passionate and hungry for him just before, her eyes full of some unearthly light that had gripped him by the throat and hadn't let go. She had never seemed more lovely to him.

Yet something had changed and he wanted to know what.

'Lark,' he repeated, sharper this time. 'What's going on?'

She was still a moment, then he heard her take a deep breath and turn back to him. Her cheeks were wet, her lovely green eyes red. 'I'm sorry, Cesare,' she said thickly. 'But I can't do this any more.'

He stared at her, not understanding. 'What do you mean? You can't do what?'

'I can't be your wife, not like this.'

A feeling of foreboding began to gather inside him. She'd touched him reverently. Kissed him as though he were precious, and no one had ever done that to him before. No one had ever held him as if he mattered, as if he was important.

But even so, there had seemed something deliberate about the time she'd spent doing it. As if she was savouring it, savouring him. Then that light in her eyes as he'd slid inside her that he didn't understand. It had looked like grief.

It was a goodbye.

He went cold all over. 'Tell me what you're actually saying,' he demanded. '*Exactly* what you're saying.'

'I can't keep sleeping with you.' She sat up abruptly and turned, slipping off the bed. 'I can't keep being… intimate with you. That has to end.'

'What?' He stared at her in bewilderment. 'Why?' And then, in a hot flare of jealousy, he scowled. 'Have you found someone else?'

'No, no, nothing like that.' She was dressing and he found it unbearable all of a sudden. He reached out over the mattress, catching her hands and pulling her back down on the bed again.

'Tell me,' he growled, turning her over and pinning her beneath him. 'Why can't you sleep with me any more? And why are you crying?'

She swallowed, her jaw tight. 'Let me go, Cesare.'

'No. Did I do something to hurt you? What?'

'Yes,' she burst out suddenly, passionately. 'You did do something. You made me fall in love with you.'

The words echoed around the room, a slow horror dawning inside him.

'Love?' he echoed stupidly.

Her eyes glittered and this time she didn't look away. 'I know you don't want it and I know you said love would never be any part of this marriage and I thought I was fine with that, but… I'm not. I love you, Cesare. I love you so much.'

This time, he was the one who pushed himself away from her as if she'd burned him, horror deepening, the anger that he'd thought he'd vanquished rising along with it.

'No, Lark,' he said in a rough voice. 'No. I told you—'

'I know what you told me.' She sat up, pain stark in her eyes. 'And don't worry, I'm not asking for you to love me in return. I know how you feel about that. And I'm not going to leave—I would never take her away from you and I'm not leaving her—but I can't keep pretending we have a real marriage when we don't.'

'Why not?' he demanded, fury abruptly running through his veins. At her for changing everything when he'd thought things were perfect, and at himself for not realising that making her happy might have had this effect on her. For not seeing her growing feelings.

Another way you're selfish. You didn't even think about how she *might feel. All you wanted was your damn new legacy.*

Yes, and why shouldn't he? He was a selfish bastard and he'd never made any secret of the fact. Yet something like self-loathing wound through him all the same.

'Because I can't.' More tears were rolling down her cheeks and for some reason the sight of them hurt, like small slivers of glass pushed beneath his skin. 'I spent my childhood loving my mother, hoping it would help her, fix her somehow, but it didn't. I don't want to do it again.'

The fury felt as if it was choking him. 'I'm not broken, Lark. Why the hell would you think I need fixing?'

'You don't,' she said passionately, wiping futilely at her tears. 'It's not that. It's just… I want to love you so much. I want to make you as happy as you made me, but sometimes I feel as if there's a part of you that you keep shut away, a part that you don't want me to see. And it's like that night again, Cesare. Where you have all of me, but I have nothing of you.'

He knew what she was talking about. The days when the pressure of trying to keep both her and Maya happy, to not give them any reason to doubt and mistrust him, got to him. Sometimes he found himself furious for no reason and always when he should have been happy. It felt as if he was missing something, lacking something, and he couldn't pinpoint what, which angered him. He didn't want her to see that, didn't want his anger to become something toxic, the way his parents' had, and so he'd shut himself away and dealt with it, only coming out again when it had gone.

She didn't need to see that. No one did.

'You do have all of me,' he insisted, fighting his anger. 'But there are some things that you don't need to see.'

'What things, Cesare? What is so very bad about you that I shouldn't have to see it?'

He gritted his teeth. He kept on telling her what kind of man he was, but she didn't seem to believe him. Perhaps he needed to drive the point home. 'You know what my parents did to me,' he said flatly. 'You know how sick they were, how they let their anger consume them. Well, I'm no different. I was furious with them after they died, for the hell they made of my childhood, and for a long time I let that fury take charge. And I nearly let it consume me the way it consumed them. But then I decided I'd had enough of letting them control the course of my life, and so I decided to break up their legacy and finally move on. Then you came along, Lark. You and Maya. And you both gave me hope that I could do something different.' He found his hands had curled into fists and he tried to relax them. 'But that doesn't change who I am. I'm what my parents made me, Lark. Angry, and bitter, and selfish. That's the part of me that you don't need to see.'

'No.' Lark's eyes suddenly burned, her voice fierce. 'No, you stupid man. You might be angry and bitter, and God, if anyone's got a right to that, it's you. But you're not selfish. You're the opposite. You put your daughter first, every time, and you're caring and kind and supportive. Why do you think I fell in love with you, you idiot?'

'It's not for her,' he insisted, an odd pain starting up inside him. 'It's for the new—'

'Legacy, yes, so you keep saying,' Lark interrupted furiously. 'But I don't believe that and I don't think you do, not for a second. You're doing all that for her, because you love her. Because *she* matters to you, not your stupid legacy.'

His heart was beating far too fast and he felt like a man drowning and trying to grab onto a life vest as it floated past. And missing.

She's not wrong.

She was, she had to be. Love was toxic. Love had killed his parents and it had nearly killed him. And he didn't want any part of it. Ever.

This time it was he who pushed himself off the bed and reached for his clothes. 'I'm not having this conversation,' he said in a hard voice. 'In fact, we will never speak of it again.'

Lark didn't move as he dressed, sitting on the bed naked and so achingly beautiful she stopped his heart.

'That's too bad, Cesare,' she said, still fierce. 'Because I can't have half-measures. I've given you all of me, but if I can't have all of you, then I have to do something. I don't know if I can do friendship, but that's all I've got to offer you right now.' Tears gleamed on her cheeks even as anger glittered in her eyes. 'I'd like to tell you I'm sorry, but I'm not.'

He had no answer to that. It was a futile argument anyway, and he knew how those kinds of arguments ended. Very, very badly.

So he said nothing and strode from the room instead.

CHAPTER ELEVEN

LARK DIDN'T KNOW what to do after that. She didn't know where that left them, she only knew that while he still believed those terrible things about himself, there was no hope for them. No hope for their marriage at least.

Eventually, her heart tearing itself apart in her chest, she slept, but he didn't join her.

And she didn't see him the next day at breakfast either. Apparently, according to one of the palazzo staff, he'd gone in to the office and didn't know when he'd be back.

Three days later, he still hadn't returned, and Lark began to wonder if he ever would.

It wasn't fair. She didn't care about herself, but denying Maya his presence was a terrible thing to do. She tried calling him to tell him so, but he wouldn't answer. He didn't respond to her texts either.

Eventually, after much thinking and then some hunting around, she found Aristophanes's private number and called him instead.

'Lark?' Aristophanes's deep, cold voice was full of surprise. 'To what do I owe the pleasure?'

Lark took a breath. 'I need you to talk to Cesare. He won't answer any of my calls and I'm getting desperate.'

'Oh?' This time Aristophanes sounded wary. 'Why?'

She swallowed. 'I…um…told him I loved him and I couldn't be his wife any more, not in the way he wanted, and we argued. Then he left.'

'Oh, dear,' Aristophanes said, his voice very neutral. 'That does sound…difficult.'

'He seems to believe he's some terrible person,' Lark said, fighting tears and quite unable to stop herself. 'But he's not. He's the most wonderful man I know and I just want him to believe—'

'Yes, yes,' Aristophanes interrupted, sounding distinctly uncomfortable now. 'I see your point. Well, we can't have that. I'll give him a call.'

After he'd disconnected, Lark sat with her phone in her lap, staring at it, only for Maya to come running into the salon the next moment, closely followed by Emily.

'Sorry to interrupt,' Emily said, looking apologetic. 'Maya was trying to find Signor Donati.'

Lark swallowed. Maya had been finding Cesare's absence difficult and that had upset Lark too.

'It's okay,' Lark murmured, reaching for her daughter and cuddling her on her lap. 'Why don't you take the rest of the day off, Emily? I'll look after her.'

Lark held her daughter's warm little body after Emily had gone, rocking her gently while Maya curled up against her.

Every part of Lark hurt. Every part of her ached. She couldn't let it break her, though. She couldn't afford to be broken, not for Maya's sake. And if Cesare didn't return? Well, she'd fill in the gap he'd left in her daughter's life. Maya had started out without a father and luckily she was young enough that she'd forget him if he never returned.

If this was what life was like from now on, then so be it. She would endure for her daughter.

But she wasn't going to love again, that was for certain.

Cesare was the only man for her and always would be.

Cesare sat in his office in the Donati Bank building in central Rome, a nearly empty bottle of whisky sitting open on his desk, the couch he'd been sleeping on for the past few days still covered with the blanket he'd found from somewhere.

He hadn't been back to the palazzo. He missed his daughter and his wife so badly it felt as if he'd lost part of his soul.

But he couldn't go back, not now. He'd thought he could keep Maya and Lark safe from him, from his anger and his selfishness, but it was clear that he couldn't.

He'd hurt Lark, he knew. He'd made her cry. And he wished he could go back and soothe her, comfort her, tell her he'd never hurt her again, but he couldn't promise her that.

Because he would. She loved him and he couldn't bear that, not when love always ended in destruction. Far better he steer clear of both her and Maya for the foreseeable future. That seemed to him to be the only way forward.

He poured the rest of the whisky into his glass and sipped at the fiery liquid.

Why couldn't she have kept it to herself? Why couldn't she *not* have fallen in love with him? He couldn't give it back to her and eventually that lack would fester, and then who knew what would happen? She had a fiery temper and love could turn that toxic.

You know it wouldn't. She's nothing like your mother.

Maybe, maybe not. There were no guarantees.

Love ruined everything.

His phone was sitting on his desk, the screen full of missed call notifications from Lark. He hadn't contacted her since he'd walked, mainly because he had no idea what to say to her, not when the only things he could think of would hurt her and badly.

Just then his phone buzzed, but it wasn't Lark this time. It was Aristophanes.

Reluctantly, Cesare answered it. 'What?' he demanded gracelessly.

'I see,' Aristophanes said, as if something had been confirmed for him. 'You're sulking.'

Cesare glowered at his office windows, at the sun sinking over his ancient city. 'I am not. Why are you calling me anyway?'

'Because your lovely wife asked me to.'

Cesare's heart contracted. 'Why did she do that? I didn't ask her to.'

'I know you didn't.' There was the faintest hint of censure in his friend's tone. 'She's desperately worried about you. Apparently she told you she loved you and you left.'

His jaw felt tight, all his muscles tense. 'I had to. You know my past. You know that I can't—'

'I know that you're lying to yourself,' Aristophanes interrupted mildly. 'And I know you're being a coward.'

Cesare growled. 'I had to leave her. She seems to think that I'm this paragon and I'm not. I never have been.'

'No,' Aristophanes agreed. 'You're not a paragon. But you're not as bad as you seem to think you are. And anyway, it doesn't matter what you think. She's the one that really matters to you and I think you know that.'

Deep inside, something shifted painfully in his chest. 'It's my legacy that matters,' he said, but even to himself his voice sounded uncertain. 'Not her.'

'What did I say about lying to yourself?' Aristophanes said. 'You think I didn't see the way you looked at her at Maya's birthday party? Your heart was in your eyes every time. You're in love her, you fool. And I think you're telling yourself any lie you can get your hands on so you don't have to admit it.'

'No,' Cesare said hoarsely, even as the truth settled down inside him and wrapped around his heart, filling him with an icy terror. 'No, that's not true.'

'It is,' Aristophanes said, relentless. 'You're in love with her and you're afraid. And I know why.' He paused. 'You're not like your parents, Cesare. You do know that, don't you?'

'Do I?' His voice sounded strange. 'I am angry for what they did to me. I thought I was past that, but I'm not. And I can't trust myself around Lark or Maya when I'm angry because—'

'Because what? You think you'll harm her? Harm Maya?'

He stayed silent, frozen all the way through, the terror of that thought robbing him of speech.

'No,' Aristophanes went on calmly. 'You wouldn't. You're not that kind of man and you never have been.'

'You don't know that.' His voice had gone hoarse.

'I do,' his friend said. 'And if you won't take my word for it, take Lark's. She's a smart woman and she's in love with you, and I don't think that would have happened if you'd been anything like your parents.'

Cesare took a breath, and then another, fighting his fear.

He'd always told himself he was a selfish man, but part of him had always known that was a defence. A defence against caring. Yet all the lies in the world hadn't stopped him from caring for Maya. And he knew, in a sudden flash of insight, that they hadn't stopped him caring about Lark either.

He'd told himself that making Lark and Maya happy was for his legacy, but that was a lie too.

He was making them happy because he loved them. He loved his daughter, and he loved his wife. He loved them so much it hurt. And he was terrified of it. Terrified that he was just like his parents…that love would turn him into someone he wasn't. Someone toxic and violent, who would hurt those he cared out.

There was a silence down the other end of the phone.

'What if you're wrong?' he said hoarsely. 'What if I really am just like my father? Or my mother?'

'Don't be ridiculous,' Aristophanes said briskly, because he'd always been uncomfortable with emotion. 'You haven't killed anyone yet that I know of.'

'Ari, don't—'

'Cesare, stop. Your parents ruined your childhood, it's true. But you don't have to let them ruin your future. You have a beautiful daughter and a lovely wife. Be a shame to throw all that away because you're not brave enough to man up.'

Cesare shut his eyes.

His friend was right. He was giving in to his fear, letting them ruin his life the way they'd always done.

His beautiful, courageous wife had set him an example. She'd had a child on her own, had loved her and cared for her despite her own doubts. She'd created a wonderful childhood for her—she hadn't let her own run her life—and then she'd moved with him to Italy, sacrificing the life she'd made in England for Maya and for him.

She'd shown him what love was. That it didn't have to be toxic or destructive, or full of rage and pain. She and Maya had shown him that love was happiness. Was laughter and joy and wonder and awe. It allowed for anger and hurt, gave space for those emotions, yet didn't allow them to linger or fester. Love allowed for honesty. Love allowed for fear.

How could they give him all of that and he give them nothing in return?

His love for Maya had been instant and irrevocaable and he'd had no control over it. But Lark had been different. She'd slipped under his guards and wrapped herself around his heart and now he couldn't get rid of her. She was there for life.

And he didn't want to get rid of her. He wanted her to stay there for ever. Doing anything else would *really* make him like his parents.

'Sorry,' he muttered to his friend. 'I have to go.'

'I thought you might,' Aristophanes said.

And laughed.

Lark was sitting in the salon, her books on the table in front of her, trying to study when Cesare suddenly burst through the door.

His hair was standing on end, his shirt half undone. He had no jacket and no tie, and he looked as if he hadn't slept for a week.

He was also the most beautiful sight she'd ever seen.

She pushed herself to her feet, her heart beating suddenly very fast. 'What are you doing—' she began, but didn't get any further, because Cesare had crossed the distance between them without a word, pulling her into his arms before she could finish.

'I need to tell you something,' he said roughly. 'I've been a coward and a fool, and you will never know how sorry I am for running out on you the way I did.'

Lark put her hands on his chest, aching at the feel of him, at the familiar warmth of his body surrounding her. 'Cesare, what are you doing?'

'I'm coming home.' The look in his eyes burned. 'I'm coming home to you, because I love you, Lark Donati. I've loved you since that night we spent together, I think, but I told myself it was only physical. Because I was afraid. Afraid of my anger. Afraid of love. Afraid that I would become like them. I didn't want to fall into the same traps of emotion, to love someone so much it became an obsession and then hatred.' He took a shuddering breath. 'I didn't want to end up hurting you or Maya.'

Lark's eyes filled with tears, her heart full and painful in her chest. 'You wouldn't. You *never* would, Cesare. I told you that you're nothing like them, *nothing*. Because what they did to you and to each other wasn't love.'

'Yes,' he breathed. 'Yes, I think I'm beginning to see that.' His arms tightened around her. 'And I'm beginning to see what love actually is, and you taught me that. Love isn't an ending. It's a beginning. It's creation. It's joy and happiness, and my life here at the palazzo. My life ever since I married you. Love is you, Lark. You and Maya.'

Her throat hurt and she could feel tears start to slide down her face, but they were happy tears. Joyful tears. She touched his face. 'So what does that mean?'

'It means, little bird, that I want you to be my wife for real. I want to be faithful to you, to love, honour and cherish you, in sickness and health, until the day I die.'

Lark smiled, aching with love for him. 'In that case, I do.'

And that's what they did.

Lark never remembered that night they spent together, but it didn't matter.

She lived it every night, in Cesare's arms, for the rest of their lives.

EPILOGUE

'It's twins,' Aristophanes said. He sounded…angry.

Cesare bit back a smile. 'Congratulations?'

His friend had called him in a fury, because apparently he'd found out that a woman he'd spent a night with three months earlier was now carrying his child. Two children, to be exact.

'I don't need your congratulations,' Aristophanes snapped.

'I fail to see what you're so angry about,' Cesare said patiently. 'Weren't you supposed to be trying to get her pregnant?'

That had been the case, according to Aristophanes, but he had refused to give Cesare any details. Annoying. Especially because Aristophanes had always made it clear he didn't want children.

'Don't you understand?' Aristophanes growled. 'I can't *not* have them in my life. They're mine.'

'I don't think you really want me to say I told you so, do you?'

Aristophanes said something filthy in Greek then disconnected the call.

Cesare put his phone back on his desk and smiled.

Just then, the doors of his office opened and his wife

came in. She was wearing the most beautiful sea-green gown, the exact shade of her eyes. It wrapped around her figure deliciously and he wondered if perhaps they could change the time of their dinner date. Maya was with Emily; she was taken care of. They could make it later. Give him some time to—

'Cesare,' Lark said, looking stern. 'No, we don't have time, and anyway…' The stern look faded to be replaced by the smile she gave for him and him alone, the one that lit her face, that made him ache to hold her. 'I have something to tell you.'

It couldn't be bad, not judging from her smile, yet his heart started beating faster all the same. 'Oh?' He pushed his chair back and got to his feet, coming around his desk to where she stood and taking her gently into his arms. 'Something good, I hope?'

Her face shone. 'I'm pregnant.'

It *was* something good. It was the best news he'd ever had.

And a little under eight months later, when Lark delivered their twins, a boy and a girl, it got even better.

He realised then what he'd subconsciously known the day he'd chosen Lark and his child over his own fear.

That the true Donati legacy was love and always had been.

* * * * *

If Italian Baby Shock *left you wanting more, then make sure to check out the next instalment in the* Donati Heirs *duet, coming soon!*

And why not explore these other dramatic stories from Jackie Ashenden?

Pregnant with Her Royal Boss's Baby
His Innocent Unwrapped in Iceland
A Vow to Redeem the Greek
Enemies at the Greek Altar
Spanish Marriage Solution

Available now!